For Warren Frazier, and for Moses Cardona

JOYCE CAROL
OATES
DADDY LOVE

A Mysterious Press Book
for Head of Zeus

First published in 2013 by Mysterious Press,
an imprint of Grove/Atlantic, New York.

This edition first published in the UK in 2013 by Head of Zeus Ltd.

9 7 5 3 1 2 4 6 8

A CIP catalogue record for this book is available from the British
Library.

ISBN (HB): 9781781850657
ISBN (TPB): 9781781850664
ISBN (E): 9781781852477

Printed in Germany.

Head of Zeus Ltd,
Clerkenwell House
45-47 Clerkenwell Green,
London EC1R 0HT

www.headofzeus.com

I

APRIL–SEPTEMBER 2006

1

YPSILANTI, MICHIGAN
APRIL 11, 2006

Take my hand, she said.

He did. Lifted his small hand to Mommy's hand. This was maybe five minutes before the abduction.

Did he see their car? she asked him. Did he remember where they'd parked?

It was a kind of game she'd played with him. He was responsible for remembering where they'd parked the car at the mall which was to teach the child to look closely, and to remember.

The car was Daddy's Nissan. A silvery gray-green that didn't stand out amid other parked vehicles.

He was an alert child most of the time, except when tired or distracted as he was now.

Remember? Which store we parked in front of? Was it Home Depot or Kresge Paints?

Mommy narrowed the stores to two, for Robbie's benefit. The mall was too much for his five-year-old brain.

He was staring ahead, straining to see. He took his responsibility for the car seriously.

Mommy began to worry: she'd made too much of the silly game and now her son was becoming anxious.

For he was fretting, Is the car lost, Mommy? How will we get home if the car is lost, Mommy?

Mommy said, with a little laugh, Don't be impatient, sweetie! I promise, the car is not *lost*.

She would remember: the lot that was often a sea of glittering vehicles was now only about one-third filled. For it was nearing dusk of a weekday. She would remember that the arc lights high overhead on tall poles hadn't yet come on.

The harsh bright arc lights of Libertyville Mall. Not yet on.

It was in a row of vehicles facing the entrance to Kresge Paints that she'd parked the Nissan. Five or six cars back. The paint store advertised itself with a festive rainbow painted across the stucco facade of the building.

The Libertyville Mall was a welcoming sort of place. As you approached the entrances, a percolating sort of pop-music emerged out of the very air.

Didn't trust her spatial memory in these massive parking lots and so Dinah never walked away from her car without fixing a landmark in her memory. A visual cue rather than trying to remember the signs: letters and numerals were too easy to forget.

Unless she jotted down the location of the parked car on a scrap of paper, which she had not done.

Searching for the car Robbie was becoming increasingly fret-ful. Tugging at Mommy's hand in nervous little twitches. And his little face twitched, like a rabbit's.

She assured him: I'm sure the car is just over there. Next row. Behind that big SUV. Perpendicular to the paint store.

Robbie was straining to see. Robbie seemed convinced, the car was *lost*.

And how would they get home, if Daddy's car was *lost*?

Mommy asked Robbie if he knew what *perpendicular* meant but he scarcely listened. Ordinarily new and exotic words were fascinating to Robbie but now he was distracted.

Mommy what if . . . Lost?

Damn she regretted the silly parking-lot game! Maybe it was a good idea sometimes but not now, evidently. Too much excite-ment in the mall and Robbie hadn't had a nap and now he was fretting and on the verge of tears and she felt a wave of protective love for him, a powerful wish to shield him, to clutch him close and assure him that he was safe, and she was safe, and the car was only a few yards away, and not *lost*. And they were not *lost*.

Except: when she came upon the row of vehicles in which she was sure she'd parked the Nissan, it wasn't there.

Which meant: she'd parked in the next row. That was all.

It's right here, Robbie. Next row.

You must hide from your child your own foolish uncertainties.

You must hide from your child your own sudden sharp-as-a-razor self-loathing.

Dinah was thinking more positively—(a good mother is one who insists upon thinking "more positively")—what a good thing it is, that a child's fears can be so quickly dispelled. Robbie's anxiety would begin to fade as soon as they sighted the car and would have been totally forgotten by the time they arrived home and Daddy came home for supper.

And Daddy would ask Robbie what they'd done that day and Robbie would tell him about the mall—the items they'd bought, the stores they'd gone into, the plump white pink-nosed Easter bunnies in an enclosure in the atrium at the center of the mall and how he'd petted them through the bars for it was allowed for visitors to pet the bunnies as long as they did not feed them, or frighten them.

PET ME PLEASE DON'T PINCH ME.

And Robbie would climb onto Daddy's lap and ask, as he'd asked Mommy, Could they have an Easter bunny? And Daddy would say as Mommy had said, Not this year but maybe next year at Easter.

And to Mommy in an undertone, Jugged hare, maybe. With red wine.

Pulling Robbie through a maze of parked vehicles and certain now that she saw the Nissan, parked exactly where she'd left it, Dinah was prepared to say in relief and triumph: See, honey? Just where we left it.

2

"Please take my hand, Robbie."

He did. He lifted his pudgy hand to Mommy's hand, and she squeezed his fingers. Between Mommy and the five-year-old passed a shivery sort of happiness.

Apophatic came to her mind. That which is *beyond words*.

So much in motherhood she was discovering is *beyond words*.

"Do you see our car? Daddy's car? Remember where we parked?"

The car was Daddy's 2001 Nissan sedan. Cool green-gray of the hue of weathered stone.

On their outings together, Mommy used such opportunities to instruct Robbie. It was Mommy's intention that their son would not be a passive child like so many in this electronic-media era but a child actively involved in whatever Mommy was doing that had some reasonable learning-purpose to it.

And Robbie definitely helped Mommy locate stores on the mall-map, for his five-year-old brain was quick to coordinate colors, and quick to match names and numerals with patches of color, as in a board game.

Robbie had been "responsible" for remembering the location of the car when Mommy parked, since the age of three.

He was a quick bright sweetly docile boy most of the time—given to happy chattering. A nonstop barrage of questions for Mommy and Daddy—*Why? Why? Why?*

The flood of speech had begun when he'd been two. In three years, Robbie's vocabulary and *way with words* had developed considerably.

And it was a task, to get such an active-minded child to sleep through the night. Often waking at 3:30 A.M. and coming to their bed claiming he was *all slept-out, so it must be morning.*

Mommy was asking gently: "Remember? Which store we parked behind? Was it Home Depot or Kresge Paints?"

She'd narrowed the stores down to two, for Robbie's benefit. The mall was somewhat overwhelming to him and shopping here left him both excited and fatigued.

"Home Depot or—Kresge Paints?"

Robbie stared, strained to see. Robbie was taking his responsibility for the car seriously.

This was a game and yet not entirely a game. Now Dinah began to worry that she'd made too much of it and if Robbie couldn't locate the car he'd be disappointed in himself, and upset.

The downside of an active-minded child is that he sets high standards for himself, if but unconsciously. And it should not be a five-year-old's self-judgment that he might *fail.*

8

Shopping with Mommy Robbie was like a little bird fluttering its wings—so much energy! And so much to look at, and question! *Mommy what's this? Mommy what's* this? A display of plump white pink-nosed Easter bunnies in the mall had thrown him into an ecstasy of excitement. He'd tugged at Mommy so hard that her arm was aching. She'd joked to friends, as to Whit, that she was becoming asymmetrical—a slight stoop to her right shoulder, from leaning down to their little boy.

He was a happy child. He was not a fretful, whimpering or whining child. Yet, sometimes when he was frustrated, particularly by a task he'd presumably learned to do, or by some accident having to do with the toilet, Robbie burst into tears of disappointment, hurt, rage. The *woundedness* in a five-year-old's face! It would require a Rembrandt to render such exquisite subtlety, such pain. At such times Dinah was in awe of the child.

For at such times he seemed to her not *her child*, but *the child*.

Robbie was saying in a worried voice that their car wasn't where it was supposed to be—was it? The car was "lost"—was it?

And Mommy said no, the car was definitely not lost—"Just wait a minute. Maybe we'll see it in a minute."

Robbie was asking how they would get home, if the car was "lost"?

"Sweetie, don't be so impatient. I promise, the car is not *lost*."

Recalling how, as a child, she'd been subject to little spells of anxiety about being *lost*.

All children must feel this anxiety in some way. *Lostness* as a condition of which no one can speak clearly for it is a mystery—the *lostness* deep within the soul.

Dinah would remember that the lot, often a sea of glittering vehicles, was only about one-third filled at this time, nearing dusk of a weekday. She would remember that the lights high overhead on tall poles hadn't yet come on. There'd been a *mistiness* to the air that made her vision seem blurred and her senses less alert than usual. And yes, she was tired.

Tired was what she'd never admit to her husband, let alone her son. *Tired* was her secret shame, alarm, disappointment in herself for she believed that *tired* was just ordinary weakness. *If you are happy in your life and living a good life you are not ever tired but suffused with the strength of happiness.*

She wasn't a religious person. Yet, in the deepest region of her soul she would say *Yes I believe.*

Whit would laugh at her. Whit laughed at such clichés. Whit laughed at weakness not his own.

It was facing the entrance to Kresge Paints she'd parked the car. Five or six rows back. The paint store advertised itself with a rainbow painted across the stucco facade of the building.

Didn't trust her spatial memory in these big lots and so she never left her car without fixing a landmark in her memory. She preferred a visual cue rather than trying to remember the signs: letters and numerals were too easy to forget unless she wrote them down.

Though she did remember, the car was in Lot C.

Robbie, over-excited by the mall, each window display having drawn his attention, and some of the displays (electronics, toys, sports gear) having stimulated a barrage of questions to put to Mommy, seemed to have forgotten Kresge Paints though, when they'd left the car, Mommy had pointed to the gala rainbow facade. Too much had intervened, evidently. Too much to look at. Robbie was tugging at Mommy's hand in nervous little twitches. And his little face twitched, like a rabbit's. She wanted to kiss him, he was looking so perplexed; at the same time so *responsible*.

At such a juncture a cruel parent might have said *It was your responsibility to remember where the car was parked. If you can't find the car we are lost and have no way of getting back home.* But she was not a cruel parent and she would never have said such a thing.

Though her own mother might have said such a thing to her when she'd been Robbie's age.

Not seriously of course but as a joke. Dinah's mother liked such jokes.

Don't go there! Back up.

"Honey, the car is over there, I think. Behind that SUV. We can't see it just yet but—it's perpendicular to the paint-store entrance. OK?"

Robbie was uncertain. Robbie was straining to see.

"The paint store? With all the colors? The car is there."

Robbie shook his head—his forehead crinkled in worry—the car *was not there.*

"Robbie, wait. Stop pulling at me, please! The car *is there*."
Dinah had to smile. Though a child is small, a child is *strong*.
But the fact is, an adult must always be aware: a child is *small*.

It was easy to forget this simple fact sometimes. When she and
Robbie were together for an uninterrupted period of time—in
the car, or at home; watching videos, reading a storybook ("reading" what was Robbie believed he was doing though Mommy
knew he'd memorized the words to his favorite stories from having them read to him many times); when he was sitting with her,
and they were almost of a height; or Robbie was sitting on her
lap, which made him seem taller. Or Robbie was chattering and
she was laughing and half-listening and thinking, as the child's
father had observed, that there was something about their son's
personality that made you think he was your size, essentially.

And quick, and smart. Fascinated by words.

"'Perpendicular.' D'you know what that means, sweetie?"
Impatiently Robbie shook his head *no*.

"It means, like, an *L*"—Mommy made a shape with her hands,
to indicate perpendicularity—"one thing is going this way, and
the other is going this way. See?"

Robbie nodded uncertainly. He was looking anxiously about
for the car—where was the car? *Why couldn't he see the car yet?*

Firmly Mommy gripped the pudgy little hand and walked
forward in the direction of the car she'd parked only an hour
before, making her way between parked cars, waiting for a lone
vehicle to pass with headlights shining faintly, gripping the anxious child's hand and just slightly annoyed now, not so much

with Robbie but with herself, for encouraging this silly game as a way of strengthening the child's memory, or his sense of responsibility, which she was thinking now hadn't been a good idea maybe; or, if a good idea originally, not so great an idea now. It frightened her, sometimes seeing young mothers lose control and scream at their small children in the mall, or in the vast parking lot; there was something about the anonymity of the mall that seemed to encourage such outbursts; and sometimes the young mother shook her child, and you could only stare in horror, you could not look away from such private, devastating moments; but you must shield your child from seeing, and so you did—you hurried away—no backward glance . . .

The good thing was, of course Robbie's anxiety would vanish in another few seconds, when they found the car (which wasn't exactly where Dinah had thought it was, after all; must be the next row, and not this row) and Robbie would soon know, and a few minutes later Robbie would have totally forgotten his anxiety for in a five-year-old emotions rise and fall like gusts of wind. She would say, in triumph: "See, honey? Right where we left it."

But she was stammering. Words like bits of concrete or chalk in her mouth. Trying to say *I can't remember.*

I guess—I can't remember.

We were almost at our car when something hit me—the back of my head—it seemed to fall from the sky like a large bird—like a swan—it was just above me and beating me with its wing—but the wing was sharp like a sword . . . Then I was gone.

*I was gone, and Robbie was taken from me. I felt his fingers
wrenched from my hand . . .*

*I was gone and could not scream for help but it was like I'd been
pushed into the water, and came up again, to the surface, and somehow I was on my feet—I don't know how I managed to get up but
I was on my feet—I guess I was running after them—him?—I was
screaming and I was running after the SUV—I think it was—or a
van—he'd gotten Robbie from me and into the van—it happened so
fast—they said it was a concussion from the first blow—when I was
on my feet—now I could scream and I was screaming at them—at
him—I was stumbling after the van—we were at the end of a
row of parked cars, the lot was emptying out—nobody seemed to
see us—I was running after the van screaming and then somehow
it happened, I couldn't see for the blood running into my eyes, the
van was turned around—the driver had turned it around—he was
going to run me down—I could see his face—I could see his grinning
teeth—his whiskers—some kind of a hat, a baseball cap maybe,
pulled down low over his forehead, and he was wearing glasses—dark
glasses—his eyes were hidden behind those dark reflector glasses like
motorcyclists wear—and I guess—I wasn't going to step aside—I was
screaming for Robbie and that was all I was thinking about—the
van wasn't going fast yet and I thought—must have thought—that
I could grab the door handle or pound on the windshield with my
fist—I could get Robbie back, I thought—and—I guess—he aimed
right at me, he ran me down . . .* She wouldn't remember being
dragged beneath the van fifty feet in the parking lot and the van
lurching and skidding to shake her off until finally her body fell

loose and was flung aside like a sack of laundry and when the first witnesses arrived she was lying seemingly lifeless on the pavement—in utter astonishment having seen a woman struck down by a van and dragged beneath it across the pavement for fifty feet and her body finally released. *And the van left the lot, sped up and left the lot, we'd just come out of Home Depot and were too far away to see who was driving the van or what color it was or the license plate, we ran to the poor woman lying there broken-looking we were sure had to be dead.*

3

"Take my hand. Please, Robbie!"

He did. He took her hand.

In the mall he'd become over-excited and hadn't always obeyed Mommy unless she raised her voice but now in the confusion of the parking lot the five-year-old was subdued, apprehensive.

She would think *The first of the mistakes.*

"Are you tired, sweetie? We'll be home in a half hour. Help Mommy find our car, OK?"

It was his responsibility. This was the game. Robbie loved games because (usually) Robbie was good at games.

"See it yet? It's somewhere up ahead."

The game was to allow Robbie to lead *her.* Tugging at her hand to hurry *her.*

But Robbie wasn't sure where the car was. Too much had happened in the mall to intrigue him and dazzle him and he'd wakened early that morning and naturally he was tired, and inclined to be fretful and anxious. And she could hardly say in exasperation to a bright energetic five-year-old *Didn't I tell you, you'll be sorry if you don't take a nap?*

It was hard for Dinah to scold her son. Hard for Dinah to scold anyone.

Even when, at Story Hour at the local public library, it was her dear son Robbie who sometimes chattered and jostled other children, he was so *enthusiastic.*

Or when, feverish with excitement, Robbie slipped his hand out of hers inside the mall and ran on his short stubby legs to the Easter bunny enclosure paying no heed to Mommy calling after him with exasperated laughter.

The mall was a favorite place for mothers with young children. There was a children's play area and there were numerous "outdoor" restaurants serving inexpensive food. Each season had its appropriate decorations—Christmas had lasted a long time at the mall; and now with the approach of Easter, fluffy white bunnies were displayed amid pots of bloodred tulips and vivid-yellow daffodils. Some of the mothers seemed to be herding as many as three—four?—young children and these women Dinah regarded with awe. How could they manage, with more than one child! Robbie was as much as she could handle, or could imagine wishing to handle. All of her volcanic Mommy-love was invested in this single child. Whit was possibly less obsessed with parenthood than Dinah, but not by much less.

Imagine, if Robbie was twins! a friend had said and Whit had said wittily *You mean he isn't?*

"This way, honey. I think we want to go in this direction."

Robbie had been tugging impatiently at her hand. He must have forgotten Kresge Paints though Mommy had pointed out the garish rainbow facade as a landmark for locating the car.

With a fraction of her (distracted) consciousness she'd been aware of the vehicle, a van, that passed her and Robbie slowly as if the driver was looking for a place to park as close to Home Depot as possible. She'd gripped Robbie's hand to allow the van to pass before they stepped out from between two parked vehicles and in that instant her awareness of the van was no more distinct than her awareness of any other vehicle, stationary or moving, within her range of vision. She did not see who was driving the van, or whether there was someone sitting in the passenger's seat. She might have been aware that the van wasn't a new shiny model but a not-new slightly battered model of the indefinable hue of last fall's leaves trapped in gutters and ravines. She was certainly not aware of the van's license plates either front or rear.

"Watch out, sweetie *Do not ever* step out from between parked cars without looking *left and right*."

In the mall she'd allowed her little boy to become over-stimulated. It was the indulgence of a young mother intoxicated with motherhood as with an exotic drug.

She'd shared in his excitement. It was a giddy experience to see the world through a child's eyes. For she could not remember ever having been *so young*.

Before bringing Robbie to the mall, initially in his stroller, she'd never quite realized how fascinating the displays were in many of the store windows and in the mall's three-storey atrium, beside the escalators. (And the escalators were like amusement park rides, thrilling to the very young, and seemingly very safe.) So much in this consumer paradise was gaily colored and in motion to catch the eye's attention and to hold it.

She understood: the mall was designed to draw in shoppers, consumers. The children's displays were designed to draw in children whose parents might be prevailed upon to buy them what they begged for. She and Whit did not "believe" in impulsive buying, certainly not at the whim of a five-year-old. Nor could they afford to spend money on perishable toys or things that Robbie would quickly outgrow.

Yet there was an undeniable romance to the mall. Ridiculous, the glamour of new-model auto vehicles positioned on revolving platforms, that quite dazzled the eye. The very names were seductive—*Forester, Wrangler, Optima, Cavalier, Echo, Lancer, Sunfire.* Whit complained of the Nissan he'd had for years. It was time to buy a new car, maybe a SUV. They might look ahead to driving their kid with other kids to—soccer games? Little League softball? (Whit was one who'd long scorned suburban life yet each year was sinking a little more into it as if into, as he liked to say, a spongy AstroTurf.) They'd need a vehicle larger than a sedan. But not probably new: "pre-owned."

Yes. There was something undeniably thrilling in children's faces at the mall as they tugged at their mother's restraining hands.

Mom-my! Mom-my! MOM-MY!

Robbie could be headstrong and even defiant, in an environment that was both disorienting and enchanting. The glittery Libertyville Mall was an environment distinctly *other*, set beside which the household in which he lived with Mommy and Daddy was altogether ordinary.

Whit had read to Dinah a passage from one of his psych texts: at age two the average *Homo sapiens* is as "wantonly destructive" as he/she will ever be.

They'd laughed together. Grateful that their son was a special child who hadn't been "wantonly destructive" or even, in fact, unusually difficult, as a toddler; and, by age three, had already begun to show signs of child-maturity—allowing other children to go first in line, curbing his instinct to interrupt, expressing embarrassment for his mistakes. Especially, Robbie was inclined to be deeply embarrassed if he spilled or fumbled something. But when he was tired, or in an edgy mood, Robbie reverted to his younger toddler-self, a tight-wired little creature on the verge of a tantrum.

The Libertyville Mall was just too large. It must have been miles they'd walked—drawn irresistibly forward by something glittery and promising in the near distance. Dinah had known exactly what she'd wanted to buy and in which (probable) stores and yet, once at the mall, you were captivated by the bright buoyant welcoming Muzak and forgot your resolutions. And the boy was fatigued, and not thinking clearly.

In the parking lot Mommy was thinking *In another minute he'll see the damned car! Then, all will be happy again.*

She was thinking of how, aged two, Robbie had had a bronchial infection; his skin was flaming-hot, his temperature was a stunning 102.2°F. In a panic she and Whit had driven him to the ER in Ann Arbor—Whit hadn't wanted to wait for an ambulance—he'd driven the 1991 Nissan sedan so fast it began vibrating and shaking as if it had been about to disintegrate into pieces and Dinah had clutched at their small limp feverish son vowing *If You will save him, dear God, I will never doubt You again. Please God help us, Robbie is so little and we are so helpless.*

In the ER, emergency medical workers had started an IV line in his arm. And how small Robbie's arm, and how small the "butterfly needle" used to draw blood! The chief resident had said *Your son has a bronchial infection and is severely dehydrated* and she hadn't wanted to think that he had spoken to her and to Whit with an air of reproach or disgust. *Dehydrated? What was that, exactly? Not enough water? But how do you make a two-year-old drink water if he doesn't want to?*

Later she'd clutched Robbie's hand. When Robbie was in intensive care. The bronchial infection had invaded both lungs. The child was so very small in the (child-sized) hospital bed. Family members had come but weren't allowed to stay because the room was too small. Dinah's mother had come and stood in the hall wringing her hands. A hag's face like something hacked out of stone. Yet she'd seemed genuinely stricken, and sorry for what she'd said about Dinah's marriage to the "mulatto disc jockey" who was Perry "Whit" Whitcomb whom Dinah adored.

Someone has to be to blame, if a two-year-old is critically ill. Such an illness as a severe bronchial infection doesn't just happen. Dinah's instinct was to say *It was my fault. I didn't realize he wasn't drinking enough liquids.* She had known that Robbie's skin was hot, that he was running a fever, but her pediatrician had told her repeatedly that babies run fevers, babies sniffle, snuffle and fret and cry, she must resist the impulse to fly into a panic at every snuffle. Yet she'd stammered to anyone who would listen *It was my fault. My fault.* As if her confession might mitigate the child's condition. As if God might decide not to punish the child, but the (bad) mother. It had been gallant of Whit to object saying *It's my fault just as much, Dinah. It's both our faults. And it happened fast—overnight.*

Gallant of Whit to say *We're amateurs at this. We're trying to learn. But Robbie is going to get well. And Robbie will never remember a minute of it.*

Dinah wondered if this could be so: Robbie wouldn't remember the eight-day vigil in the University of Michigan Medical School Hospital in the children's wing.

Young children remember very little. Unless the corollary was more likely: young children forget very much.

Lacking a concept of *death, extinction* they are not able to attach emotions to such possibilities.

Robbie had recovered. Of course, Robbie had recovered.

He was susceptible to lung infections, severe colds. But he'd recovered and they were sure he didn't remember and he'd never known that his parents had been desperate with fear that he might die; that they'd sat on either side of his narrow little bed and clutched at his small perfect hands and wept together and laughed and reminisced *When he was conceived? That night? I'm sure it was that night—you know—at that terrible "motor hotel" in Bozeman—in the morning a swarm of blackflies rushed at us— ugh!—in our hair, eyes, mouths* . . .

In such ways you are bonded with another. The connection with the man was so deep, and the connection through the child, she could not ever separate herself from them, no more than she could separate herself from her own soul.

She shuddered at such thoughts. But it was a shudder of an almost uncontainable joy—was it?

"Robbie? Our car is in the next row—I promise. Please don't *cry.*"

One witness would report to police officers that the little abducted boy had seemed to be crying in the parking lot. He'd been pulling at his mother's arm and she'd been speaking urgently to him. Asked if she'd overheard what the mother was saying to the boy the woman said no, she'd been too far away. She'd been headed into Home Depot, not coming out.

Witnesses who'd seen the mother and the child inside the mall as recently as fifteen minutes before the abduction would tell police officers *There was nothing special about them. There was nothing that would make you look at them.*

A young mother with her little boy. Nice-behaving and nice-looking but nothing special.

The little boy seemed excited about the rabbits. But all the children were.

And there didn't seem to be anyone harassing them or following them, that I noticed. Nobody suspicious.

A sudden cry seemed to erupt out of the air. Not a plea for help but sheer sound—surprise, terror.

She'd have thought it was Robbie but it was not Robbie but herself.

What struck her seemed to come down vertically, from a height above her head. She'd seemed to see—(it was happening far more swiftly than she could fathom)—a large bird with flailing wings, a ferocious bird, like the bird that tore out Prometheus's liver, and in the next instant she was falling, and Robbie's fingers were wrenched from hers even as the child screamed *Mommy!*

4

Take my hand, she said.

How many times a day she said. When they were *out*.

And he'd taken her hand for he was an obedient child.

And she'd clasped the little hand tight for she was Mommy, and she was responsible.

In the mall, he'd slipped away from her more than once. Squealing and giggling, he'd slipped away from Mommy who'd had to run after him.

But that was a game. Out of a game erupts childish laughter.

If he was tired, if he was fretful, she'd have liked to push him in the stroller but he was too big for the stroller now, he said. And he was too big to be carried in Mommy's arms! He said.

He was a bright chattery happy child. He was (sometimes) mischievous and exasperating and in bed his poor Daddy moaned pulling a pillow over his head *Oh Christ! The little rooster is crowing already.*

Daddy liked to tell funny stories of how mischievous Robbie was and of how lively Robbie was waking Daddy and Mommy in the middle of the night wanting it to be morning because morning was breakfast-time and a happy time before Daddy left. And if it was a day that Mommy had classes, he'd be taken to day care and left at day care where there were children he liked but some children he did not like—(why, wasn't clear. Dinah had made inquiries).

He'd given her his hand. They were approaching Lot C.

She'd had no preparation. She'd had no warning. No sixth sense or Mommy-instinct.

It was a pit of confusion into which she fell headlong. She was aware that she was very likely dying because her breathing had ceased because her skull was cracked because her soul was leaking through the crack like smoke from abandoned, long-smoldering mines in Pennsylvania that yet continue to ascend through cracked pavement. There was time to think of this—yet there was no time—for what happened, happened so swiftly. It would be said that she'd managed to rise from the pavement bleeding from a head wound and she'd managed to stumble after the van into which her son's abductor had thrown him, like an automaton she must have stumbled after the van for she had little conscious memory of it, of screaming, not fear so much as rage, white-hot rage, and she was clawing at the vehicle, she was trying to grab hold of a door handle; and then, the van reversed, and sped at her, and she stood her ground in defiance and the impact was such, her soul seemed to have been struck from her body, like her breath. And when she came to consciousness in a brightly lighted place smelling of something sickening, antiseptic it might be, alcohol, they were asking who'd taken her son, what could she remember of the attack and the abduction, and she was trying to stay awake to tell them what she could but her jaw had been broken, teeth had been knocked from her jaws and words failed her.

Yet she knew to be conscious of the terrible loss.

The child's hand snatched from hers. Mommy had had to *let go.*

This was the defeat of her life as a mother. The defeat of her life as a human being. Though they were telling her that none of this was her fault—of course.

Her son had been taken. Whit's son.

There had been no ransom demand so far. Very likely, it had not been a kidnapping.

And, "Police in three states are looking for the abductor. There's every kind of media coverage."

She was being prepped for more surgery. Her body was a smashed starfish. She smiled down upon it, pitying.

Patient going down. Distinctly she'd heard these words as she sank into sleep.

5

Later, it might have been another day. There was no Time in this place where she was no longer Mommy but the pitiful broken thing with half a face scraped off.

Everyone was very kind. The nurses were soft-spoken, very thoughtful and kind. She faded in and out of consciousness and in and out of caring if she lived, or did not live.

Her last effort had been to throw herself at the van. Stupid, and a fiasco. If she'd had more sense she would have walked the child directly to the car parked perpendicular to the front entrance of Kresge Paints, she'd have walked on the sidewalk and not taken what had seemed to be a shortcut through the parking lot, slantwise, through a labyrinth of parked cars; she would not have made herself so vulnerable, and put her child at risk.

Her last effort. A failure.

She'd been struck down by her assailant with a blunt instrument, believed to have been a hammer. Dragged beneath her assailant's vehicle for fifty feet along the parking lot pavement. Both her legs had been broken, her right arm, ribs and collar-bone broken; the skin on the right side of her face had been torn away; teeth were missing in her lower and upper jaws. She'd been an attractive young woman and now would have a *Hallowe'en jack-o'-lantern face.*

She had no need to look at this face, yet. She knew.

In morphine delirium she'd consoled herself what good luck it was, Robbie couldn't see his mother now. He'd have shrieked at how grotesque Mommy had become.

In the street sometimes he'd stared at handicapped people, especially children. His eyes widened in an expression of childish fright utterly empty of sympathy or identification.

As he'd stared in wordless horror and revulsion at a squirrel struck by a vehicle in the street near their house, not quite dead, writhing in the gutter.

Don't look, honey. Shut your eyes.

She said to her husband in an urgent voice as if what they were discussing—what she was discussing with him, not quite comprehensibly—was a concern of, say, the next several hours. That she would wear a "nice pretty white satin" mask when Robbie came to see her, so Robbie wouldn't be frightened of her. Of all things they must spare their son seeing his mother so mutilated.

Me instead of him. If only.

It was a ridiculous notion. It was a profoundly naïve notion.

For the abductor had not wanted an adult woman but a young child. That was the point of the abduction—the *young child.*

Whit would appear on TV. An unshaven man with pleading eyes, disheveled grayish brown hair. The man's skin was pallid and yet distinctly the skin of a "mixed-race" individual. (Black? Native American? Middle Eastern?) Photos of five-year-old Robbie would appear on TV.

The father was *Whit Whitcomb.* His 11 P.M.-nightly-except-Sundays program on WCYS-FM *American Classics & New Age* was one of the NPR station's most popular programs. At the present time a substitute was taking Whitcomb's place.

Whit would be interviewed on WCYS-FM and make his special appeal as the Ypsilanti police had encouraged him. Whit Whitcomb whose sexy radio-voice was dazed now, somber and faltering.

If anyone knows. Anyone, anything. Missing five-year-old Robbie Whitcomb. Taken from the Libertyville Mall.

The mother was not available but *hospitalized, in critical condition.*

It was broadcast in the media that the mother had been struck by the abductor in his van. It was known that the abductor of her son had tried to kill her.

Would you love me if you heard me on the radio and had never met me?—Whit had more than once asked Dinah.

Yes! Absolutely.

And she'd asked him: Would you love me if you'd just heard my voice?

Whit laughed saying, Sure.

Just my voice and not me? You'd have loved *me*?

Sure, kid.

This had been a long-ago time. Before the baby.

Or maybe she'd been pregnant then. Married just four months and pregnant lying asprawl in their bed listening to Whit's taped program as they often did. The thrill of her husband's deep-throated radio-voice, sexy, kindly, playful, confiding *And now we turn to something ex-quisite in this 1945 recording of Billie Holiday singing "What Is This Thing Called Love."*

This was the riddle. This was the hard question. What is this thing—*love.*

Mommy had not been Mommy for much of her life. Before that she'd only been "Dinah"—she'd never understood how free, how undefined, how *slight* her identity, before she'd become pregnant and had her baby.

She'd been a half-person, all those years. No wonder she'd been lonely!

Yet her mother, having *had her,* had not been happy. You could not say that Dinah's mother was a *whole person.*

Now, there was never a time when she was only Dinah. Now, she was Mommy whose name happened to be "Dinah"—but this wasn't the most important part of her identity.

Does a woman go a little crazy, having a baby? Do you get used to the baby? Do you *want* to get used to it? When Dinah recalled her life before Robbie, her life before the pregnancy, she was astonished at how inconsequential she'd been: just her.

She'd fallen in love with Perry "Whit" Whitcomb when she'd been twenty-three. She had never been in love before and had been overwhelmed by the experience and yet: it was not the kind of nurturing love, the kind of *desperate* love, you felt for a child.

That happy time. Even "problems" had been pleasurable, then.

It was a different time now. There was nothing luxuriant in their love now. They were not brash and young now. The Mommy was twenty-eight years old and the Daddy was thirty-four years old and they would not ever be young again.

Through her broken jaws she tried to speak. Tried to ask *Have they found Robbie?*

Whit told her no not yet. *Not yet* was Whit's way of consolation.

At her bedside Whit radiated calm. Elsewhere Whit was crazed.

Whit cradled her in his arms. As much as he could lean over the bed, without hurting her. (But could she feel pain? It was a cotton-batting sort of pain, a roaring in her ears that might have been screams but were muffled.) He loved her very much, he said. Their son would be found and returned to them, he was certain.

Whit did not tell her the latest news. For the latest news was usually no news. A day, a day and a night, two days, several days, a week and finally twelve days—and then, fifteen days: no news.

There was a good deal of mistaken news. Sightings of the boy with his abductor. Sightings of the "beige" van.

The mother was being kept alive by IV fluids. She was no longer on a respirator but she was still being fed artificially. Her nourishment was called *Mechanical Soft*.

Twenty-nine days in the Ann Arbor hospital and two weeks in a rehab clinic learning how to walk again. And yet—Dinah would never walk normally again.

Her skull had been badly fractured. She'd bled into her brain.

It was a *miracle* she'd lived. A *miracle* she'd ever managed to stand on her feet let alone walk again.

She would continue rehabilitation for months. Her sense of balance was askew. Often it would seem to her that the floor was tilting below her or the very sky tilting above her. She would never sleep through a night—never more than a few hours before waking frightened and disoriented. The child's fingers were gripped tight in hers and she would never let go.

Do you love me anyway? she'd asked Whit. It had become a soft-fading wistful mantra.

Jesus, Dinah—I love you more than anything and anyone in my life. I've always loved you, kid.

Robbie's father had gotten high soon after they'd brought their infant son home from the hospital. Smoking dope exhaling smoke luxuriantly through his nostrils saying, God damn, Dinah, we're going to bring up our son to be *happy*. None of this bullshit from our families, OK?

She was totally in agreement. No bullshit from any quarter.

No neurotic crap. No "complications." Our beautiful son is perfect in his soul, all we're required to do is let him flower. Stay out of his way.

She was totally in agreement.

She did not believe in a god of vengeance and wrath—a petty little ranting god. She believed in a god of whom it might be said humankind had been made in this god's image—this was the god Robbie would know, if Robbie knew any god at all.

Already, Robbie had asked about "God"—he'd been hearing the word and all strange words provoked his curiosity. *Mommy what is "God"?* uttered with such childish perplexity and a wish to be informed that she'd laughed and kissed him and said *God is a spirit in the universe looking over us. God is in this house but invisible.*

"*Invisible?*"—Robbie asked.

You can't see God. When there's something you can't see it's "invisible."

"*'Visible—how do you know where it* is?*"*

Dinah and Whit had quoted their remarkable son how many times. There was never a son like their Robbie to say such clever things.

"*'Visible—how do you know where it* is?*"*

One night when Dinah was still in the hospital at Ann Arbor Whit didn't come to her room until late.

After 10 P.M. he came. His words were slurred and his breath smelled of beer. He began to cry. She asked if there was news and he said no news and that was why he was crying. He'd been strong until now but now he was falling apart he said. Hid his head in his arms, on Dinah's hospital bed. His face hidden against her thigh. The damp of his tears wetting the bedclothes. He kneaded her bruised hand. She was confused and not entirely conscious. She'd come to hate the morphine for what it did to her mind but she wasn't able to sleep without it. Or maybe she was asleep and was dreaming a dampness against her thigh and a man sobbing beside her saying softly so that no one could hear *Why! Why'd you take him there. Why'd you let him go.*

6

CHURCH OF ABIDING HOPE
DETROIT, MICHIGAN
APRIL 12, 2006

Shall we not say, we are created in God's image?

Gently the Preacher moved among the flock of starving souls. His blessing fell upon them like precious seed. His eyes bore deep into theirs, in knowledge of their aloneness and their great hunger which only one of the Preacher's spirit could satisfy.

Moses Maimonides tells us that Time is so precious, God gives it to us in atoms. In the smallest units, that we may bear them without harm to ourselves.

For we dare not gaze into the sun. For the sun will blind us.

It is the Preacher who gazes into the sun, and risks harm for the sake of the faithful.

We are a dignified people. We are not a crass cowering cowardly people but a great people, of these United States of North America. We are a people created in God's image and we abide in the great mystery of all Being.

Shall we not say that we cannot know the limit of our grace? That we cannot plumb the depths of our own single, singular souls, let alone the depths of God?

Knowing only that we are brothers and sisters in Being— beneath our separate skins.

The Preacher spoke in a voice of consolation. The Preacher spoke in a voice of tenderness, forgiveness. The Preacher spoke in a voice that did not judge harshly. The Preacher spoke in a voice acquainted with sin.

The Preacher did not stand at the head of the flock and preach to uplifted faces but moved between the rows of seats in the central and side aisles of the little church with the ease and grace of a true shepherd. Often the Preacher reached out to touch a shoulder, a head, an outstretched hand—*Bless you my brother in Christ! Bless you my sister in Christ! God loves you.*

The Preacher was a visitor at the Church of Abiding Hope. He had several times given guest sermons here in the small asphalt-sided church at the intersection of Labrosse and Fifth Street in the inner-city of Detroit in the shadow of the John Lodge Freeway.

The congregation of the Church of Abiding Hope—some seventy-five or eighty individuals of whom most were over fifty and only a scattering were what you'd call *young*—gazed upon the Preacher in a transport of incomprehension. It was *white-man's* speech elevated and wondrous as a hymn of a kind they rarely heard directed toward them and yet in the Preacher's particular voice intimate as a caress.

Understanding, their own minister Reverend Thomas Tindall could provide them.

The Preacher was a tall man of an age no one might have guessed—for his stark sculpted face was unlined, his eyes quick and alert and stone-colored in their deep-set sockets, his beard thick and dark and joyous to behold. His mouth that might have been prim and downturning was a mouth of smiles, a mouth of beckoning.

The Preacher's words were elevated but his eyes sparked. *My brothers in Christ. My sisters in Christ. God bless us all!*

The Preacher wore black: for the occasion was somber. A black light-woolen coat, black trousers with a sharp crease, black shoes.

The Preacher wore a crimson velvet vest: for the occasion was joyous. And at his neck a checked crimson-and-black silk scarf.

The surprise was, the Preacher was not dark-skinned like the faithful of the Church of Abiding Hope or Reverend Tindall who was the Preacher's host. The Preacher's skin was pale and bleached-looking and if you came close, you saw that it was comprised of thin layers, or scales, of transparent skin-tissue, like a palimpsest. The Preacher was the sole *white face* in the church and bore his responsibility with dignity and a sense of his mission.

The Preacher's rusted-iron hair that was threaded with silver like shafts of lightning fell to his shoulders in flaring wings. Parted in the center of his head that was noble and sculpted like a head of antiquity.

The congregation stared hungrily perceiving the Preacher as an emissary from the *white world* who was yet one of their own.

The Preacher spoke warmly of the great leader W. E. B. DuBois who exhorted us to see the beauty in blackness—*In all of our skins, and beneath our skins. The beauty of Christ.*

The Preacher spoke warmly of Reverend Martin Luther King, Jr. who exhorted us to never give up our dream—*Of full integration, and full citizenship, and the beauty of Christ realized in us as Americans.*

Then in an altered voice the Preacher spoke of his "forging" years in Detroit for he'd been born in this city that was beloved of God even as it was severely tested by God.

Forged in the rubble of the old lost neighborhood south of Cass and Woodward. In the rubble of destroyed dreams. Now there were small forests of trees pushing through broken houses. Gigantic weeds and thorns pushing through cracked pavement. The very house of his childhood. His father had worked in the Fisher Body plant long since closed. His grandfather had worked at the Central railroad station long since closed. These mighty buildings, fallen to ruins. The grandeur of Woodward Avenue, fallen to ruins. The tall buildings of Bellevue Avenue, fallen to ruins as in an ancient cataclysm. Yet the spirit of God has not forsaken Detroit. His spirit prevails here and will rise again. A strange and wondrous landscape of colors, flowers, vegetation, birds. Feral creatures breed here. Pollution has given to brick walls a beautiful sepia tint. Shattered glass on roadways shines with the grandeur of God. You might think that God has forsaken Detroit but you would be mistaken for God forsakes no human habitation, as God forsakes no man. The great Christian leader John Calvin said, Nature is a shining garment in which God is concealed but also revealed.

The Preacher was of this soil, for he had been born on the first day of the troubles of July 1967 when Detroit, long smoldering, had erupted into flames.

The Preacher had been born to his mother in a house on Cass Avenue. The Preacher had been born into a time of "racial" troubles and yet—the knowledge is in us nonetheless, *we are blessed.*

For the flaming city on the river had been an emblem of the black man's deep revulsion for his place in these United States, which had been then a place of ignominy and ignorance—deception and duplicity. God had sent flames to reveal this injustice. God was the burning city as the God of the Old Testament had been the burning bush. No one could shut his eyes against such a revelation.

Decades had passed since then. Much had changed since then.

In a bold voice the Preacher spoke. In the voice of one who knows.

And now in the new century it was prophesized, the races would rise together. There would be a dark-skinned President in this new century—the Preacher had had a vision, and the Preacher *knew.*

To all this the congregation listened mesmerized. Scarcely did the congregation draw breath. Of what they could comprehend they could not believe a syllable of such a fantastic vision and yet, in their souls they did believe.

All that the Preacher extolled to them, they did believe.

The Preacher was concluding his sermon. The Preacher was visibly shaken by his own words. On the Preacher's palimpsest-skin there shone sparkling tears.

My sisters and brothers in Christ, we are borne upon a vast journey in uncharted seas. I am not one who provides you with easy answers to your doubts but I am one who tells you, you are beautiful souls and from beauty there issues beauty everlasting.

From my heart to yours, my dear sisters and brothers in Christ, I say to you *Amen.*

Through the church came joyously spoken *Amens.*

The sermon had ended. The Preacher stood to the side, at the pulpit. As the choir began to sing—"I Love to Tell the Story"— "When I Survey the Wondrous Cross"—"There Is a Balm in Gilead"—the Preacher sang with the choir in his deep resonant voice.

Now it did seem that there were younger members of the congregation. At least one-third of the choir was comprised of shining young faces.

At the conclusion of the service Reverend Tindall clasped the Preacher's hand. Tears brimmed in Reverend Tindall's glaucoma-dimmed eyes. His face was of the hue of cracked leather. His scalp was shiny-dark, with a fringe of fleecy white hair. He was a vain old man and yet insecure and well intentioned. You could see that he was very proud of his friendship with the eloquent white preacher.

Thank you, Brother Chester! That was what this congregation was thirsting to hear.

The Preacher was invited to stay for supper with the Reverend and his family. But the Preacher explained he could not stay that night. He was *in transit* for he was badly needed elsewhere.

There is always terrible *need*. Sometimes I think we dare not lay our heads down to sleep, or we will lose all that we've gained.

The Preacher was given to such pronouncements, grave and matter-of-fact. It was not always clear what the Preacher's meaning was, yet you did not doubt that the Preacher knew.

You will come back to us? Brother?

Of course I will come back to you, Brother. In my heart I will not depart.

The collection of $362 was divided between them—Reverend Tindall and the Preacher who was known to the Reverend as Chester Cash.

In the alley beside the asphalt-sided church the Preacher's van was parked.

The van was dark as an undersea creature. Even its windows were dark-tinted. On the roof of the van was a wooden cross painted a luminous white and secured with ropes and on this was written in crimson block letters

T

H

E

CHURCH OF ABIDING HOPE

U

S

A

The van was a 2000 Chrysler minivan and its chassis dented and scarified but it appeared to have been recently painted. It had been recently painted in some haste for there were smears of iridescent dark-purple paint on several of the windows like fingerprints.

From the threshold of the Church of Abiding Hope, you could see the van parked in the alley. But you could not see into the van for the windows were tinted.

It must have been that the Preacher had no family remaining in Detroit for he had not sought them out and did not seem to wish to speak of them now. When Reverend Tindall asked after the Preacher's mother, the Preacher glanced downward and replied in a murmur—Weeping may remain for a night, but rejoicing comes in the morning.

Reverend Tindall asked after the Preacher's ten-year-old son who'd accompanied the Preacher to the Church of Abiding Hope the previous spring.

The Preacher frowned as if trying to recall this son. As if just perceptibly startled by the question.

Nostradamus has chosen another pathway, it seems. He has gone to live with his mother and her people in the Upper Peninsula.

A fine boy, Reverend Tindall said. You had said, your son would follow you into your ministry?

He was but a child then. He has not put aside childish ways. And he dwells now among Philistines—it is his choice.

The Preacher spoke sadly yet not without a shiver, a twitching of whiskered jaws, as if the memory of a young son's betrayal were fresh to him, and painful.

Reverend Tindall seemed about to ask another question about the lost son but then thought better of it. For the Preacher was breathing quickly and stroking his whiskered jaws unsmiling.

By His light, the Preacher said in a lowered and quavering voice, I walked through darkness.

Brother, Amen!—Reverend Tindall clamped the Preacher on his shoulder.

Because the Preacher was a frugal man, and chose to spend his money solely on necessities, he lived in the minivan much of the time when he was *in transit*. In the van he kept clothes, books and documents, a miniature kerosene stove, canned food. It was a part of the Preacher's ministry to visit small churches across the country and to deliver guest sermons where he was welcomed. Abiding Hope is a family, the Preacher said. We are brothers and sisters in Christ. We are one, inside our skins. Everywhere, we recognize one another.

As he stood on the threshold of the little asphalt-sided church on Labrosse Street, Detroit, speaking with Reverend Tindall in the early evening of April 12, 2006, the Preacher glanced at the van parked in the alley a few yards away. His deep-socketed eyes encircled the van. Clearly there was something about the van, its very stillness, its iridescent-purple chassis and the surprise of the luminous white cross secured to its roof, that riveted his attention.

Brother, are you sure you can't stay the night? Or at least have supper with us?—Reverend Tindall seemed disappointed. His glaucoma-dimmed eyes blinked and blurred.

The Preacher thanked him kindly. The Preacher had now the keys to his van in his hand. With a wide smile the Preacher explained that he was bound for the West Coast, for Carmel, where a new ministry in the Church of Abiding Hope awaited him.

7

I-80 EAST
MICHIGAN, OHIO
APRIL 13–14, 2006

Take my hand, he said.

But the child would not.

I say to you, son—*take my hand.*

When the quivering child did not lift his hand, did not obey, Daddy Love seized the hand, and squeezed the little fingers with such force, the smallest finger audibly cracked.

Inside the gag, the child screamed.

On I-80 east a continuous stream of vehicles.

On I-80 east Daddy Love drove at just slightly below the speed limit taking care that the white-painted wooden cross on the roof of his vehicle wouldn't be shaken by wind and blown off. He was a patient driver who took little note that vehicles were constantly passing him. In the wake of enormous trailer-trucks, the Chrysler minivan swayed slightly.

Like souls passing, Daddy Love thought. The stream of vehicles.

He was among them and yet elevated. It was Daddy Love's particular destiny that amid the mass of humankind only a very few like him were possessed of the power to *see*.

Eastern religions believed in the "third eye"—in the forehead, just above the bridge of the nose. Through meditation, through zealous religious practices, the "third eye" opened and vision flooded the brain.

Daddy Love was one of these. From boyhood he'd been gifted with such visions. Like the power of X-rays to see through flesh. Daddy Love *saw*.

It was a particular insight of the brain. An activated and excited area of the brain just behind the eyes. The frontal lobe, it was called. Neurons *fired* in mysterious surges like heat lightning soundless in a black summer sky.

But such scientific terms, mere *words,* meant little to Daddy Love who understood how *words* were purely invented and how if you were a master of *words,* you were a master of men.

Ordinary individuals could not understand. Ordinary individuals comprised somewhere beyond 99 percent of *Homo sapiens*.

You had to suppose that the Buddha achieved enlightenment, and so Nirvana—(or maybe that was the Hindu heaven not the Buddha heaven)—at about the age of Daddy Love when he'd been, in that long-ago lifetime, a gangling boy named Chester Czechi who'd first *seen*.

He'd known he was a special case. He'd known that he would be forever a pilgrim in his life, embarked upon a (secret, thrilling) pilgrimage, utterly unguessed-at by others.

Even his family. Especially his family.

(Daddy Love smiled, recalling. He had not seen his fucking "family"—fucking "relatives"—who'd betrayed him to the Wayne County, Michigan, juvenile authorities, aged twelve, in twenty-six years.)

Now on the interstate highway what the ordinary eye saw wasn't the Chrysler minivan but the luminous white cross secured to the van's roof.

The cross was approximately four feet in height. The horizontal plank was approximately three feet.

The cross did shudder in the wind. But Daddy Love, who was a natural-born carpenter, a visionary with a talent for *using his hands,* had secured it tight, with both wires and rope.

The cross was a curiosity: some observers might smile. (In recognition of the sacred cross, or in condescension that a cross might be so awkwardly affixed to the roof of a minivan.) Some might try to read the crimson letters hand-printed on the cross.

Most would lose interest and look away after a few seconds.

State troopers looking for a *beige, battered* van on the interstate would take little interest in this iridescent-purple minivan in the service of the Church of Abiding Hope.

Also, the van's license plates were New Jersey. The child had been taken from the Libertyville Mall in Ypsilanti, Michigan.

Daddy Love loved to be *invisible.* In the eyes of ordinary mortals and fools, the superior man can make himself so.

Spray-painting the van iridescent purple and securing the white cross to the van's roof was a means of rendering the van *invisible.*

Daddy Love had cultivated such strategies in the past. To move through life *invisible at will* you had to create distractions that drew the attention of ordinary individuals.

The ordinary individual, Daddy Love had discovered, was not so very different from a child in his perceptions and expectations. Hunting his prey, for instance, Daddy Love rendered himself close to *invisible*. He wore the clothing of an ordinary man, exactly what an ordinary man might wear to the mall on a weekday afternoon, to buy a few items at Sears, Home Depot.

A nylon jacket, unzipped. T-shirt, jeans or work-trousers. Not-new and not-expensive running shoes.

On his head, a baseball cap. But not a team cap. No discernible color, maybe gray, or beige.

The whiskers were conspicuous, that was a fact. But the whiskers were of a pale powdery-gray color they had not been at the Libertyville Mall and the tinted glasses hiding the eyes rendered the eyes invisible and unidentifiable.

(He'd heard, on the van radio turned low, the bulletin-news. Child-abduction-news out of Ypsilanti, Michigan. "Breaking news" it was breathlessly called. Had to laugh to hear a witness report how, in the mall, a few minutes before the child was taken, the witness hadn't seen anyone watching the mother and child—*no one suspicious.*)

Witnesses never get it right. Witnesses see only what their eyes see, not what is *invisible*.

Once. Daddy Love had wrapped white gauze and tape around his (left, bare) leg to the knee and hobbled most convincingly on a crutch. An old ruse of Ted Bundy's and immediately recognizable to an enlightened eye but the foolish trusting eye of a young mother who'd brought her eight-year-old to a playground—in Carbondale, Illinois—hadn't recognized it. *Excuse me ma'am could you help me—I'm having trouble getting this trunk open—damn crutch gets in the way . . .*

Hunting his prey at the Libertyville Mall, Ypsilanti. Here was the Midwest. He'd never have risked Ann Arbor which was where the university was, and not really the Midwest for everyone there was from somewhere else or was bound for somewhere else. But Ypsilanti was the very heart of the Midwest: a *nothing-place.*

He'd hunted his prey at the mall for several days in succession. He'd had a premonition, one of his *boys* was being prepared for him, soon.

Both inside the mall, and outside, he'd hunted. And inside again. Mixing easily with other Daddy-shoppers for he was in no hurry.

Kindly Daddy Love held open doors for young-mother shoppers with children. They were grateful murmuring *Thank you! Nice of you.*

Scarcely a glance at Daddy Love, as they passed through the entrance. Some of them pushing strollers and others gripping children's hands.

They moved on. Not a backward glance.

Of every one hundred children perhaps one interested Daddy Love in the depths of his soul. Of every two hundred children perhaps one excited him.

Of every thousand children perhaps one *very much excited him.*

Daddy Love trusted to the higher power that streamed through him, to allow him to *see.*

He would be immediately alerted: a child destined to be *one of his.*

A child who required, for the salvation of his soul, not the merely adequate birth-parent, but a parent like Daddy Love.

The hunt was thrilling. The hunt was ceaseless. The hunt was one in which Daddy Love participated, *invisible.*

In public places: malls, city squares, amusement parks, camping sites and hiking trails, beaches. Rarely near schools, for such territories were dangerous.

And rarely playgrounds of course. (With a few exceptions over the course of twenty-five years.)

The best time for the hunt was late afternoon shading into dusk. Before lights came on. Before the eye quite adjusted to the fading light.

People were tired then. Young mothers, their shoulders sagging.

Daddy Love was quietly thrilled by the hunt. Daddy Love was not ever impatient or agitated but passed among ordinary individuals as if he were one of them.

Except Daddy Love was not one of *them.* He'd never been!

Daddy Love ceaselessly, ingeniously inventive. Daddy Love had invented the Preacher, for instance.

The Preacher's dark garb, with the surprise of the Preacher's crimson vest and neck-scarf. The Preacher's grave and gracious manner, the blessing of the Preacher's fingers, and the Preacher's joyful smile.

Daddy Love was younger than the Preacher, for sure. Daddy Love was not so self-regarding and so pious. Daddy Love liked to joke, and the Preacher had never been known to joke.

Daddy Love considered the Preacher in the way that you might consider an uncle who's good-hearted and sincere and just not *cool*.

If women touched the Preacher's hand, or drew their fingers along his arm, or leaned to him, to smile, to murmur in his ear inviting him to have dinner with them, the Preacher did not quite know how to respond except with a stiff smile. But Daddy Love knew.

The Preacher was intriguing to Daddy Love, but only for a limited period of time. The Preacher did make money, upon occasion. You could not lock eyes with the Preacher's gravely kindly gaze and not feel the urge to open your wallet to him for in giving money to the Preacher you are giving money to Jesus Christ Himself—so it seemed. Yet with relief Daddy Love tore off the Preacher's clothes, folded them and put them away in his trunk, in the rear of the van. With relief Daddy Love shook and shimmied in his body, loose-limbed as a goose, a younger guy, a guy with a sly smile, a guy who grooved to rock music, rap music, a guy you'd like to have a drink with.

Daddy Love was a man whom other men liked. And certainly, a man whom women liked.

Children, too. Boys younger than twelve.

Daddy Love was that restless American type. Except he'd settled (more or less) in the East, or the Midwest, he'd have looked like a rancher in Wyoming. Or a (slightly older) hitch-hiker making his way to the West Coast.

Daddy Love couldn't say was he happiest in motion, in his van, which he'd painted and repainted several times since its purchase, traveling east or traveling west on I-80, or was he happiest once he'd come to rest for a while, a few months at least, maybe a year, once he'd established a home-site. Wherever Daddy Love was, there was his kingdom.

Such strategies of evasion, flight, and escape! No ordinary individual could hope to understand.

Son you are coming home!

Soon you will be home, and safe.

Son d'you hear me? I think you do son.

Daddy Love loves YOU.

Through the countryside of Ohio, Pennsylvania, and across the Delaware River into New Jersey, these many hours, hours bleeding into hours, Daddy Love never ceased to address the child behind him, in the rear of the van.

Daddy Love is bringing you to your true home for Daddy Love is your true Daddy who loves YOU.

Inside the ingenious Wooden Maiden the child made not a whimper.

Inside the gag, not a muffled cry.

Daddy Love was a stern daddy and yet loving. He'd taped a split to the little broken finger. Child-bones heal quickly but must not heal crookedly.

The child would learn quickly: each act of disobedience, however small, would be immediately punished. *No exceptions!*

Zero tolerance!

And when the child obeyed, and was a true son to Daddy Love, immediately he would be rewarded with food, water, the comfort of Daddy Love's strong arms and the gentle intonations of Daddy Love's voice. *This is my son in whom I am well pleased.*

Quickly then the child would learn. They all did.

He'd read of "conditioning"—the great American psychologist B. F. Skinner and before him the nineteenth-century Russian Ivan Pavlov. But his natural instinct was to reward, and to punish, in such a way as to instill love, fear, respect for and utter allegiance to Daddy Love in the child-subject.

The child was to be played like a musical instrument. Sometimes gently, and sometimes not-so-gently. For Daddy Love was always in control.

When he'd first sighted the child in the mall he had estimated that the child was about four years old. For Daddy Love, this was a quite young child.

By the age of eleven or twelve, the child was less desirable. The child was a pubescent. Daddy Love had little patience with pubescents and still less with adolescents.

The younger the child, the more desirable. Though Daddy Love did not want a *baby*—hardly! In any case, a baby was too much effort. A baby required a female as a caretaker.

An older child had obvious disadvantages: he would remember much of his old family, that would have to be cast off.

This child in the mall, happily chattering as he petted plump white nose-twitching Easter bunnies in an enclosure, was unusually alert, bright, and talkative. Daddy Love had been quite *ravished*!

But, how ordinary the mother.

Not coarse and vulgar like some. The woman's face wasn't luridly made up and her hair was a decent drab-brown brushed back behind her ears and her ears weren't studded with a half-dozen glittering piercings. She wore jeans but not "skinny" jeans. She wore a belted sweater that looked hand-knitted. (The belt was twisted in back, which gave her a disheveled look of which she was blissfully unaware.) Her body was slender, stringy. She had no hips and virtually no breasts. (How had she nursed her baby? Her milk would be watery, curdled. This was not a *mother*.) She wore sneakers. On the third finger of her left hand she wore a plain silver wedding band advertising *Yes! Believe it or not, somebody married me.* She was perhaps thirty years old and not getting any younger: when her face wasn't smiling, "lit up" by the most banal Mommy-love-and-pride, it was a frankly tired face. The husband would soon be unfaithful, if he hadn't been already. Who'd want to climb into bed, sink his dick in *that*. For the woman was clearly ordinary, and hardly fit for the radiant child.

The child's skin was "white"—yet the child's hair was very dark, kinky-curly. Daddy Love felt a thrill of discovery: was this a *mixed-race child*?

Daddy Love had never appropriated a *mixed-race* child. And Daddy Love was no racist.

He'd trailed them in the mall. He'd been patient, and not-visible.

In JCPenney, in Macy's, in Sears, and in the atrium at the center of the mall. The Easter-bunny enclosure that drew children like moths to flame.

Daddy Love's shrewd practiced eye glanced quickly about—in such places, where small children are gathered, laughing, talking shrilly, with (usually) just a single parent nearby, and that parent (usually) the mother, you will often find, indeed Daddy Love invariably found, solitary men of (usually) middle age, standing at a little distance, not too near, not too *visibly near*, observing.

Daddy Love wasn't one of these. Daddy Love was no *registered sex offender*.

Trailing the mother and child outside the mall Daddy Love had known that his mission was just, and necessary, and could not be delayed, when he'd seen the mother pause and fumble in her sweater pocket for—a pack of cigarettes! And quickly light up a cigarette, as the child stood innocently by; several quick deep inhalations, as if the toxic smoke were pure oxygen, and the woman desperate for oxygen; then, with a gesture of disdain, casting the cigarette from her, onto a grassless area abutting the walkway, where other careless and selfish smokers had cast their butts.

A smoker trying to quit. Failing to quit.

A smoker who was ashamed of her weakness. And maybe it was a weakness the child's father did not know about.

It was God-ordained, Daddy Love must take this child as his own.

Daddy Love hurried to his van. He would trail the mother and the child in the lot. He would not let them out of his sight.

59

He had but a few seconds to make his move—he knew how precisely such a move had to be timed, from previous experiences. The narrow window of opportunity, as it was called, had to be coordinated with a clear field and no witnesses.

How many times Daddy Love had circled a target, borne in upon a target, but had to withdraw when a random witness appeared on the scene . . .

Taking the little boy from the mother was more difficult than Daddy Love had calculated. He'd struck her on the head with a claw hammer—hard; enough to crack her skull, he'd thought. She'd fallen to the pavement like a dead weight and yet, in the next instant, like a comatose boxer struggling to his feet, somehow the woman managed to heave herself up from the ground and stagger after him . . .

By this time he had the boy in the van. How small and light the child was, yet how frantically he struggled, like a terrified little animal! He'd shaken, punched, and struck the boy with his fist on the side of the boy's head, to calm him.

It was astonishing to Daddy Love, the mother running desperately after the van—that look in her face, and her face streaming blood.

He'd swerved the van around, to run her down. Bitch, daring to defy Daddy Love!

8

I-80 EAST
OHIO, PENNSYLVANIA
APRIL 14, 2006

You're safe with me now, son.

God has sent me to you. Not a moment too soon!

She was an impure woman, the female you were entrusted to. She was your way *in*. But only *in*.

Daddy Love is your destiny. Daddy Love will be both Daddy and Mommy to you.

From this first day and forever. Amen.

At the first exit after the Libertyville Mall he'd driven to his hiding-place. Daddy Love had scoured the area beforehand and knew exactly which hiding-place was optimum. No one would expect—no *ordinary individual* would expect—that the child's audacious abductor would remain within a few miles of the mall; the assumption was that, in his beige van, he was fleeing. Roadblocks would be set up to deter him, flashing lights, sirens. But shrewd Daddy Love was not one of those who would be stopped by police in the next forty-eight hours to be questioned.

At the hiding-place behind an abandoned Shell station two miles east of the Libertyville Mall he'd parked and secured the terrified child in the Wooden Maiden, as prepared. Again he rejoiced in the child's *lightness*—the *lightness* of his bones. Nostradamus had not ever been so *light-boned*.

As planned Daddy Love spray-painted the van a dark metallic purple. Out of the battered beige van a new and more stately vehicle emerged. He took his time, he would not be hurried. There was no need to hurry. Roadblocks were being set in place, law enforcement officers were running their sirens like foolish children in pursuit of—what? No one had seen Daddy Love head-on. Not even the woman he'd run down, in that moment of utmost clarity when the front fender of the minivan had struck her, cast her down and yet not aside but beneath the vehicle, her body to be dragged across the pavement . . . It had been a bizarre experience. If he'd known beforehand what was going to happen, he'd have enjoyed it perhaps, as a bizarre incident in Daddy Love's earthly history. But it had happened so quickly, he hadn't been prepared.

The higher power had guided him, as usual. He'd managed to swerve, skid, brake and accelerate the van, and the woman's lifeless body had been cast off, finally. *If she is dead, it is her own responsibility.*

He was wearing gloves of course spray-painting the minivan. This was a familiar task—he'd done it several times before, with the Chrysler and with other vans. There was satisfaction here. A sense of accomplishment. Invariably the new paint dramatically improved the appearance of the van.

Like dyeing his whiskers a dark mahogany hue, darker than the rust-streaked hair. But now powdering the whiskers with a pale-grainy powder, a women's face-powder, and brushing it well into the bristling hairs.

And so: he'd added twenty years to his age. Not a trim thirty-nine but a trim early-sixties. Should anyone take note.

Waiting for the paint to dry, Daddy Love ate supper: takeout from one of the fast-food restaurants in the Libertyville Mall. He had a weakness for cheeseburgers with hot chili sauce, and French fries no matter how cold.

Inside in the Wooden Maiden the child slept. A rag soaked in chloroform had been sufficient, within a few seconds, for the child was very young, and could not have weighed more than forty pounds.

Such medical supplies, and other drugs to be injected into the bloodstream, Daddy Love kept in the van, in his cache. In numerous cities and in numerous hospitals and medical centers he had contacts, usually females—nurses' aides, attendants. Sometimes they were church-contacts who worked in public health care and had access to (controlled) substances. They adored Daddy Love each in her unique way. Each thinking *Maybe he is the one! He will love me, protect me.* And where female adoration wasn't enough, of course Daddy Love knew to pay.

The chloroform he'd acquired from a woman he'd befriended at the Trenton, New Jersey, Church of Abiding Hope who was a worker at a veterinary.

As long as it isn't fatal. It's to quiet a temperamental German shepherd.

It might have been twenty years ago, when Daddy Love had not yet been fully *invisible,* and had made some blunders. Those early years and the pilgrimage newly begun.

He hadn't been Daddy Love then. He'd been Chet Cash who'd been Chester Czechi. He'd been only just released from the Wayne County Facility for Youthful Offenders, at age twenty-one.

The bastards had incarcerated him for nine years! The social-worker woman and her public-defender friend who'd represented him had argued he hadn't known what he was doing, he'd had no intention of choking to death his own boy-cousin with whom he'd been playing happily, but the bastards, the prosecutor and the Family Court judge had disliked him, and given him the maximum sentence for a juvenile. And he'd learned *You must show remorse. Grief, and remorse. Otherwise—you are the fool. You are to blame for your own fate.*

Eight months released from the facility, and he'd seen his parole officer faithfully. By now, he knew. God-damn Chet Czechi knew to play the game.

Be respectful. Be calm. Smile and say Sir!—Ma'am! Let the assholes think that you give a fuck about them.

He'd begun his travels then. His pilgrimages.

Always returning to check with his parole officer. Of course.

The child had been his first *possession*. Others had entered his life transiently, and had passed out of it leaving no memory. It was not so much different from eating a meal, having a drink—the sex-act, its explosive outcome.

But this child, a beautiful little boy of about nine with silky blond hair, long-lashed tawny eyes, had been his first. (For you would not count his little cousin. That had been a true accident.) And his first loss.

The child's little heart had just—stopped . . .

It wasn't clear to Chet Czechi what had happened. He had not *intended* for anything to happen, of this sort. He'd forced the boy to swallow Valium tablets dissolved in Coke and soon after the boy had lapsed into a comatose sleep and soon after he had—died . . .

Daddy Love still felt the loss. The beautiful blond child had been meant to be *his son*.

His techniques in those days had been crude. He'd had no clearly designated plan. He'd been impulsive, reckless. He'd taken the boy from a thick-thighed female with a snout-face and big jiggly breasts—it had been a necessity of justice to take the child from *her*.

This had happened in a roadside rest-area off I-80 west, south of Erie, Pennsylvania. Stopping for a piss Chet Czechi had been ravished with the knowledge that the child in the company of the snout-faced female was meant to be *his*—yet in the possession of a stranger.

In a similar way the Dalai Lama was chosen. He thought it was the Dalai Lama—the "reincarnated" spiritual leader of Tibet.

The Dalai Lama is born to ordinary parents. You might call them surrogate parents. When a reigning Dalai Lama dies, holy Buddhist monks go into the countryside to find the new, reincarnated Dalai Lama. They follow visions, intuition. Or maybe the newly reincarnated Dalai Lama, an infant, or a young child, draws them to him. As the Biblical Mary and Joseph had been surrogate parents, to bring Jesus into the world and to prepare him for his ministry.

The situations were not identical, but similar. In Daddy Love's case, a child was born of surrogate parents but destined to be *his son*. Already when he'd been in his early twenties as Chet Czechi he'd known this in the way that, if you add together two and two, you know the answer is four.

Invincible as math or geometry, such reasoning. The inner eye awakened, and *saw*.

What the asshole media called "abduction"—"kidnapping"— "child-snatching" was in fact a courageous act on the part of Daddy Love. The cowardly way would be to pretend he hadn't *seen*.

He hadn't intended for either to die. Not the snout-faced female and certainly not the little blond boy with the tawny eyes. Yet, this had happened.

The ways of God are not our ways. Who can comprehend the ways of God!

Since that sultry summer evening in a scrubby roadside rest-stop in Pennsylvania, thousands of miles. A continuous loop of miles interrupted by durations of *domestic life*. But the pilgrimage never ceased for the boy, you could call him the *reincarnated son,* inevitably grew older—and less desirable.

Hundreds, thousands of hours. Out of Chet Czechi's blundering hands had emerged the more steady, practiced hands of Daddy Love.

And the sedatives more reliable.

No harm will befall you now, my son. You are saved.

I am Daddy Love. I am your true daddy and you are my only begotten true son.

It was my mission ordained by God to save you from the fire.

There was a great cataclysm, a fireball fell to earth. What was "Ypsilanti" has now been destroyed. It was a preview of the Rapture. The old life has vanished, my son. There is a new life now.

Such words Daddy Love uttered, that the child in the Wooden Maiden would hear and, in time, understand. In his tireless and kindly voice he so spoke. In his caressing tender voice. In his stern-Daddy voice. In his wise voice. In his somber voice. In his joyous voice. In his grave voice. He understood that the five-year-old terrified and helpless child was not yet receptive to Daddy Love's words but Daddy Love's words would have their effect gradually, in time.

So the most obdurate rock is eroded by a succession of singular, soft raindrops, in time.

He'd opened the Wooden Maiden mask, so that the child could see (if only the roof of the minivan close overhead) and hear. A gag in his mouth and duct-tape over the gag so that the child could not scream.

The child could not cry. The child could not beg for mercy. The child could not *plead*.

Daddy Love liked pleading children, to a degree. But beyond that, Daddy Love did not like pleading children.

The Preacher was more tolerant. The Preacher was more forgiving of human weaknesses.

On the whole, Chet Cash, who was Daddy Love in his "ordinary-guy" guise, did not like craven individuals. Chet did admire the brasher boys who resisted, though their resistance brought them punishment.

The Wooden Maiden was an ingenious invention of Daddy Love. As Jesus was a carpenter, so too Daddy Love was good with his hands, and found such "handyman" work soothing. He would make of his sons apprentices in such work. A child was never too young to help his father.

The Wooden Maiden was a more evolved variant of a plainer, less attractive coffin-like box that Daddy Love had utilized years ago. It was still a kind of box, carefully constructed with hinges, locks and bolts for safekeeping, yet made of high-quality cherry-wood. In shape, the Wooden Maiden resembled a casket, child-sized, or rather more it resembled the tomb of a child-pharaoh of ancient Egypt, for its structure was elegant, dignified. In his fantasies Daddy Love enjoyed imagining what law enforcement officers would say, if ever they discovered the Wooden Maiden;

if ever they discovered Daddy Love, and drew from him his life-story.

Daddy Love knew: his life-story was worth millions of dollars. If sold to the highest bidder. A made-for-TV special on one of the fancier cable channels—HBO, Showtime. A best seller simply and tastefully titled *Daddy Love: My Story.*

Law enforcement officers would marvel—*Never saw anything like this! This man is an artist.*

The Wooden Maiden, designed to contain a child less than twelve years old, was four feet, eight inches long, and twenty-eight inches wide. Daddy Love would not ever have chosen an *obese child,* certainly!

The two parts of the Wooden Maiden were relatively independent of each other: the upper, or mask; the lower, which was most of the Wooden Maiden.

The mask opened and shut on hinges. It was not unlike the design of a casket and inside, as in a casket, Daddy Love had affixed a cushion-like padding. For a child designed as Daddy Love's son must be treated with care, kindness, love.

The mask would be kept open, so long as the child was good.

The remainder of the Wooden Maiden was more like a casket, with a top lid that opened, and locked, on hinges. The Wooden Maiden was so designed that the subject's arms were pressed against his sides, and held firm. There was no accommodation for the subject to relieve himself—unfortunately. And so the subject, in time, learned to control his bladder and his bowel movements, until such time that Daddy Love released him from the Wooden Maiden for the purpose of using the toilet.

But Daddy Love was so perceptive in his design, he'd made the foot of the Wooden Maiden several inches higher than the rest, to accommodate the subject's feet. No sprained, broken, crippled feet for a son of Daddy Love!

Son, you are safe now. Protected now.

We will be home soon. Your new—your destined—home.

You will begin the game of Forget.

You have already begun the game of Forget.

In Daddy Love's rearview mirror he saw: rapidly advancing, red light flashing, siren full-blast, a police cruiser.

Ohio state troopers. The red light suddenly appearing out of nowhere, nighttime on I-80 east about ten miles from the Pennsylvania border.

He'd recently made a stop at an interstate filling station/ restaurant. He'd filled up the Chrysler's tank. He'd gone into the restaurant to get a cheeseburger, French fries and coleslaw and giant Diet Coke takeout and was still eating his supper, in the cardboard container in his lap, when the state trooper cruiser appeared. Chewing, Daddy Love yet prayed. He ate, and prayed. Scarcely aware of his silent prayer.

In the back of the van, the child in the Wooden Maiden was utterly still. No muffled weeping, no sounds of struggle. The

Wooden Maiden was a tight embrace and the child would grow into it, in time.

Closer, ever closer the cruiser came—then, as Daddy Love had known it must, the cruiser passed him, at about eighty miles an hour.

Not a glance at *him*. The assholes were hot on the trail of—who?

Daddy Love was sweating, in his armpits and crotch. But Daddy Love had to laugh.

Always you feel a rush of dread, in such situations. Daddy Love had rarely succumbed to panic, but he'd frequently felt dread. But then the dread turned into excitement, as adrenaline rushed through his veins. Better (almost!) than sex.

And the excitement turned into laughter.

It was amusing, listening to the radio. Daddy Love kept the volume low so that the child a few feet behind him could not hear. The latest news: Ypsilanti-child-abduction still laughably touted as "breaking news."

Daddy Love was curious—coolly curious—if the woman had survived? Or maybe died?

If she survived, she'd (maybe) had a look at him, through the windshield, and (maybe) could describe him. But maybe (he halfway hoped) she'd died, which would ratchet the charges against the unidentified child-abductor up to murder, but make things safer for him.

God would make that decision. If the cigarette-addicted female lived or died—that was up to God to decide.

On the 11 P.M. news as Daddy Love crossed into Pennsylvania on a mostly deserted interstate he heard that a "suspect" had been taken into custody by Ypsilanti police.

Witnesses had "identified"—who?

Daddy Love laughed, laughed.

In a way, this was the best part of it. This triumph, and this laughter. The child was but the means to *this.*

9

I-80 EAST
PENNSYLVANIA, NEW JERSEY
APRIL 15–16, 2006

Slept in the van, upright in the driver's seat. Often in daylight
and never for more than an hour.

In the back of the van, he assumed the child slept, too.

Much of the time, in this early stage, the child slept.

Several times since they'd left Detroit, Michigan, to head
east on the interstate Daddy Love had stopped in deserted rest-
areas to look after the child. He had to clean him, and he had
to feed him. These were necessary tasks. Especially the cleaning,
the child-piss and watery excrement he wished a female might
take care of, but Daddy Love was a responsible daddy and did
not shirk his duties. In a Detroit used-clothes shop on Labrosse
he'd purchased several articles of clothing for a child including
pajamas and socks. The clothes in which the child had been
abducted were now very soiled and would be discarded soon.

Always there was the dread—a half-pleasurable shiver of
dread!—that, when Daddy Love opened the mask, the child's

face would be slack, bloodless and lifeless: not a child but a child's corpse.

For the first time since he'd taken him, Daddy Love removed the duct-tape and the gag inside the child's mouth.

The gag he would need to replace, for it was soaked with spittle and nasty.

The child gasped for breath. The child's eyes rolled in his head. Daddy Love leaned above him smiling, speaking in his soft caressing assuring voice.

"Hello, Gideon! I am your new daddy—Daddy Love."

The child rapidly blinked. His eyes appeared to be all pupil. Though he was of *mixed race,* his skin was chalky white. He did not respond at all to Daddy Love but stared at him with the blank-terror of a trapped and paralyzed animal.

"You are Gideon, son. 'Gideon' is an ancient Hebrew name, of the Bible—'brave warrior.'"

The child's former name had been *Robbie Whitcomb.* But no more.

Daddy Love brought a morsel of food to the child's mouth, to feed him. But the child seemed not to know what the food was, and it fell from his mouth, into the space behind his head.

"Gideon. You are hungry, and you are thirsty. You will obey me."

He'd had to open the larger lid, and pull the child into a sitting position. Powerfully the child stank, and had to be cleaned;

then, with infinite patience, Daddy Love tried again to feed him, morsels of the cheeseburger, and sips of the Coke.

He had mixed a tranquilizer into the Coke, which would help to calm the child, and ease him into sleep once they began their journey again. As if he sensed this, the child refused to drink.

It was as if the child's mouth had locked. His jaw-muscles had locked. His spinal cord, his limbs had locked. Daddy Love would be required to coax the child out of this panic-paralysis, but not just yet, for they'd stopped at a deserted rest-stop, and intruders might pull into the parking lot at any time.

In such places, people generally mind their own business. A child being disciplined by his daddy would not draw attention. No one would dare come near the minivan with the cross on its roof, to peer inside the tinted windows. Yet, Daddy Love knew better than to take a chance.

A slightly older child, of seven or eight, Daddy Love might have half-walked half-carried into the restroom, and into a toilet-stall and washed him brusquely at the sink. The older child would understand what Daddy Love meant when he said *If someone comes in and you make a peep I will kill you* but the younger child, in his paralysis of horror, would not understand and could not be trusted.

Daddy Love cleaned the child with wetted newspapers, flung then onto the ground. Daddy Love was breathing hard, annoyed, but smiling.

"'Gideon' is your new name, son. When we are in our new home, I will baptize you properly. D'you hear?"

Daddy Love stroked the child's head. The thrillingly curly-kinky hair, like a little bush. Daddy Love leaned over the child to touch his lips to the child's forehead which was unnaturally cold and at last the child recoiled, and began to pant, and to cry as a wounded little animal might cry.

This at least signaled a response. Resistance is a normal response, initially.

Initially, Nostradamus had *resisted*. But soon, Nostradamus had given in.

Before him, Deuteronomy.

And before him, Prince-of-Peace.

In the Kittatinny Mountains of northwest New Jersey, close by the Delaware River at the Water Gap, their bodies were buried beneath boulders "unmarked" to the ordinary eye.

Only just bones now, scraps of skin, hair, rotted clothing. Their child-brightness had dimmed. They'd become too old. Boys were irresistible, adolescents not. Eleven was the bittersweet age for Daddy Love foresaw, as Nostradamus, Deuteronomy, and Prince-of-Peace had not, that his love for them, which meant his patience with them, his caring-for them, was coming to an end.

Twelve was already too old—thirteen was repellent.

The new child was very young: five years, four months according to the news stories Daddy Love had heard. There were at least six blissful years ahead.

Never had Daddy Love seized a child so young. He'd believed that eight or nine was the optimum age. But in the Holy Roman Catholic Church it was well known by religious orders that if you secure a child before the age of seven, his soul is yours.

He had never fully understood the verse from Psalms: *Out of the mouth of babes and infants, you have established strength because of your foes, to still the enemy and the avenger.*

As Gideon was so young, so Gideon would be the more shaped by Daddy Love. His memories of his ordinary life in Ypsilanti, Michigan, would fade like watercolors in pelting rain.

Daddy Love would love this child tenderly. His other sons had coarsened and disappointed him. He would not have any barrier between himself and Gideon. As soon as they arrived safely home in New Jersey, in Kittatinny Falls he would begin his *love-campaign.*

There would be not two-ness but only one-ness.

This is my body and this is my blood. Take ye and eat.

There would be little pleasure in no resistance at all, of course. Daddy Love would expect this, to a degree. As, with the older boys, there would have been little pleasure if they hadn't fought for their lives—and a little beyond.

Gideon? Will you eat? To please your daddy.

Daddy Love pried the child's jaws open, just slightly. The child shuddered and struggled and his eyes rolled in his head in a paroxysm of panic and at that moment, headlights flooded the van—a vehicle was turning into the rest-area.

The quivering child drew breath to scream. But Daddy Love was quicker clapping his hand over the child's mouth.

Soon then, that night, crossing the high windy bridge above the Delaware River at the Water Gap, and arriving at the farm, or what remained of the farm, three miles beyond Kittatinny Falls.

Upsie-daisy, son! Climb up out of there, *come on.*

Your new home, Gideon.

Daddy Love has got you.

10

KITTATINNY FALLS,
NEW JERSEY
APRIL 27, 2006

The woman lingered in the doorway. Her eyes moved over Chet Cash like hungry ants.

Anything else you'd be wanting, Chet. Just give a call.

Sure I will, Darlene.

You got my cell number.

I do, Darlene.

It's looking pretty good here, eh? Just needed a little work.

You did a great job, Darlene. I'll be calling you.

Next week is OK, Chet. I got lots of free days. At the medical clinic, they're cutting back the cafeteria hours. So I got more time.

That's too bad, Darlene. I mean—your work-hours cut.

It's this God-damn economy. You can't save a penny. I got "credit card debt"—it's serious.

I'll be calling you, Darlene. Maybe not next week, but the next.

That back room, we can air out and clean. I'd do it now, there's still time.

No thanks, Darlene. The back room is OK as is. For now.

That's your bedroom, I guess? I was noticing from outside, the shades are all drawn.

'Cause I need pitch-dark to sleep. In the morning, the light would wake me.

I guess you're kind of a light sleeper, Chet?

In the doorway the woman lingered, folding and unfolding, and smoothing, the bills Chet Cash had paid her. (He'd paid forty-five dollars in one- and five-dollar bills. The congregation at the Church of Abiding Hope in Detroit had not had bills of larger denominations to place in the collection basket.) She'd aired out and cleaned five of the downstairs rooms of the old farmhouse on the Saw Mill Road. She'd even washed windows. Chet Cash was smiling at her but his smile didn't lift into his eyes.

She was a big-bodied female of about thirty-five. Fleshy-muscled upper arms, muscled (bare) calves, and on her feet flimsy flip-flops. Her streaked-blond hair was long and thick as a horse's mane and tied up around her head in a way you had to suppose the woman thought might be gypsy-glamorous. Her face was round as a full moon, and pug-nosed. Red lipstick on Darlene Barnhauser was like lipstick on a pig but it gave her a look of sexy-girlish insolence. And she had a smudged-looking rose tattoo on her right shoulder. She lived about three miles away in the village of Kittatinny Falls, on the River Road. Since Chet had last seen Darlene, about nine months before, she'd put on weight; though she wasn't fat or in any way soft or flaccid and she was impressively strong— she'd gone to fetch the stepladder in the old barn and carried it into the house by herself.

She'd laughed with good-natured disgust, on her knees cleaning beneath the sink, reaching to pull out, with rubber-gloved hands, a desiccated rodent-corpse.

Oh, man! Like it's some kind of mauzzo-leum in here!—she'd laughed to draw Chet Cash's attention. (Chet was sweeping the front hall. Chet wasn't given to on-your-knees housecleaning.)

Chet didn't like it, Darlene never properly dressed for housecleaning, or manual labor. Like it was a matter of female pride. A big husky girl in flowery T-shirt and pink stretch-waist slacks, that were now covered in cobwebs and dirt. She'd sweated through her clothes. Her pug-nose shone with grease. But she'd done a good job and Chet would probably call her again.

She was saying now, wistfully: Y'know, Chet—we missed you. Lots of us. Like at church, it really felt sad and kind of empty when you were gone. Rev'nd Prentiss could feel it too. Like, some kind of *spirit had departed* from our midst.

I missed you all too, Darlene. But it couldn't be helped.

I'd drive out here sometimes, just to check on the house. Make sure nobody'd broke into it, like kids vandalizing places where nobody lives. It's not a bad place. Even all gone wild like it is, and the apple orchard wrecked from last winter . . .

Her voice trailed off. Chet Cash was instructing himself *Be patient. She will leave in one minute.*

81

Saying, in a flat not-encouraging voice, OK, Darlene. Good to hear it.

See, it just needs some painting, and the roof repaired. And that stone chimney kind of going to pieces. My brother-in-law Lyle, he's a real good carpenter. He could help you, if you wanted. You want his cell phone?

Thanks, Darlene. Maybe when I get settled.

This linoleum floor in the kitchen isn't bad, is it? Once you get the grime out. And the bathtub, and toilet—I got most of the stains out. Looked like some kind of small rodent died in the toilet, the size of the bones . . . It just takes work, and not getting discouraged.

Chet Cash smiled harder. Saying, Maybe.

Anybody coming to stay with you? Like—family?

Maybe.

Nostradamus?

No. Nostradamus is with his mother.

I never met her! Where's she takin him?

Upper Peninsula, Michigan. She's got family there.

That's too bad! He's a real polite nice boy.

He was.

You and her—you're, like, separated? Divorced?

Chet Cash smiled harder. Chet Cash said not a word.

His stone-colored eyes on the woman's face.

One more minute. You have one more minute, Darlene.

So badly wanting to grab the woman around the neck, squeeze and *squeeze.*

He'd bury her with the others. Mile and a half he'd have to drag her, and he'd have to be shoveling a fucking grave for her, and he had no energy for such an ordeal so soon after the long drive from Michigan. And her family in Kittatinny Falls knew where she'd been. And he was needing to tend to the child. So calmly Chet Cash spoke.

You did a great job, Darlene. I'll call.

Thanks, Chet! Like I say, it just takes work.

Very reluctantly the woman shifted her weight in the doorway. A blush had lifted into her heavy face, you could see that Chet Cash had the ability to make her happy.

You got my cell number?—I guess you do.

Right.

OK, Chet. G'night.

G'night.

A few yards away like an irrepressible child the woman turned, grinned and waved—Good to have you back, Chet. Missed ya!

There is the need for a female. Somehow, it can't be avoided.

He watched Darlene Barnhauser walk to her car. She had the side-to-side shuffling gait of a fat child. He would not take his eyes off her until he saw her climb into her piece-of-shit Saturn hatchback, with difficulty fitting her stout body behind the steering wheel, and turn on the ignition, and depart.

All these minutes Daddy Love's excitement had been mounting. Blood like hot lava flooding the pit of his belly, his groin.

In the back bedroom, where the child awaited Daddy Love.

83

11

YPSILANTI, MICHIGAN
MAY, JUNE 2006

They waited.

Each hour of each day they waited.

The phone would ring and the message would be *Good news, Mrs. Whitcomb! We've found your son and he is—*

The choice of this next word was crucial. The word might be *well,* or *alive and well,* or—*alive.*

Just to hear that word—*alive.*

" 'Alive.' 'Alive.' "

In her scratchy voice Dinah practiced. Her jaws were not so painful now when she spoke though she still had difficulty eating and so did not eat anything that involved an agitation of her jaws.

Alone, Dinah practiced. She had her physical-therapy exercises to do and these she did religiously as required and she forced herself to walk up and down stairs using just a single crutch now. She thought *It's no worse than arthritis would be. Millions of people have arthritis.*

The landline rarely rang now. Yet, Dinah often heard it.

A single short ring, cut off. She was sure.

Her heart beat hard, as she listened. In the silence of the house it would have been difficult not to hear the phone ring and yet, she was anxious that she might miss it.

Mrs. Whitcomb? Good news! We've just got word—

It was a foolish sort of consolation and yet: her heart lifted, hearing her own scratchy voice as if it were a stranger's voice on the phone that rarely rang for it was a phone with an unlisted number and this number was known only to law enforcement officials.

Aloud she practiced the words she would someday hear:

"'We've found your son Robbie and he is—*alive*.'"

Or, "We've found your son, Mrs. Whitcomb, and Robbie is *alive and well.*"

On a cork bulletin board in the kitchen, on the refrigerator door and on a wall above the telephone were snapshots of Robbie, Robbie and his parents, drawings and watercolors of Robbie's in bright colors—Dinah stared at these countless times a day.

Alone in the house on Seventh Street, Ypsilanti. Often she was alone.

She'd had to quit her part-time job at the University of Michigan biology library. They'd given her a medical leave but it wasn't clear when she'd be well enough to return and so, in all fairness to her employers, Dinah had quit.

86

As she'd withdrawn from her classes in the education school. She'd been six credits from a master's degree in public-school science education, with a social sciences major.

Co-workers from the library had more or less ceased dropping by for there was no news to relay to them. And Dinah's physical condition—her faltering words, her poor motor coordination and scarred face—her attempt to seem *upbeat*—was just too sad.

Friends and neighbors were more faithful. Especially if Dinah was sitting out on the front porch with her laptop, furiously typing.

The Internet had not yet yielded any helpful information. But the Internet was a great abyss of information, she believed.

So many "lost" children! Their wide-eyed faces stared at her, pleading.

Some of the children's photos have been posted for years.

It was a shock to discover photos of young children who'd been abducted as long as ten years ago.

Among them *Robbie Whitcomb, five years old, Ypsilanti, Michigan. Abducted from Libertyville Mall, April 11, 2006. Witnesses reported "battered beige minivan." If you have information about this abducted child please call this toll-free number . . .*

There was a fantasy you might inhale from the Internet, that all these children—abducted, kidnapped, "lost"—were together in one place, waiting to be brought back home.

As soon as she'd been discharged from the hospital and could see clearly enough to use her computer, Dinah was obsessed with typing in Robbie's name. Her own name, and Whit's. A dozen times a day.

Checking e-mail. A hundred times a day.

Whit had cautioned her. Take care, Dinah.

You don't know what you're going to see online. There are sick people out there.

It was a risk Dinah took. Daily, hourly.

Though once she'd been appalled, sickened—she'd clicked onto some sort of public-forum Web site and there were (anonymous) individuals busily discussing the abduction of her son.

Seems like the mother lost him at the mall. Bitch told this itty-bitty child to wait for her while she goes for a smoke and when she comes back, some guy with dreadlocks is dragging the kid into a van.

The bitch should be arrested—"negligence."

Hey the mom almost got killed—got dragged under the van. She'd run after it and tried to stop it.

Bitch should've been killed. Neglecting her son like that.

Dinah had struggled up from the computer, half-fainted falling to her knees.

"God forgive me! I know—I have been a bad mother."

"Do you know where he is—really? Have you ever known?"

Her mother came to see her. Her mother had the air of a Fury of ancient times, perching on a chair in Dinah's living room. Her talons shone red.

"Your husband. Your—'exotic'—'DJ'—husband."

Dinah said nothing. The ache behind her eyes and in the region of her heart was too painful.

Her mother blamed her, Dinah knew. The loss of the grandson was Whit's fault somehow, and so it was Dinah's fault too, for sleeping with Whit before they'd been married, and then for marrying him.

Dinah's mother had long held a grudge against Whit Whitcomb who'd failed to flatter and to adore his mother-in-law as she believed she deserved. And she'd never entirely succeeded in resisting speaking reproachfully to Dinah, that Dinah had taken up with a *mixed-race individual.*

"Not that I am a racist, Dinah. I hope you know that."

Dinah nodded. Oh yes, Dinah knew.

"It's just that Whit is—well, a certain kind of person."

Not our kind, Dinah thought. That's right.

Dinah's father had been a midlevel executive at Ford Motors in Dearborn, Michigan. They'd lived in a whites-only gated community called Bloomfield Vistas in Birmingham, Michigan. Geraldine and Lewis McCracken and their little daughter Dinah who'd been sent to Birmingham Day School, not the public school. In her class there were two Chinese-American children, both brilliant; no Hispanic children, no African-American children, no *mixed-race* children.

Not our kind Dinah thought, smiling. *Thank God.*

Six years before, Geraldine McCracken had happened to observe Whit Whitcomb smoking a joint in the backyard of the little rented Ypsilanti house. Dinah's mother, who drank whiskey, and whose words sometimes slurred when she came to visit her convalescent daughter, had been incensed, outraged. Marijuana is illegal. It's a *controlled substance.*

Whit had said, mildly, Not in Ypsilanti–Ann Arbor, it isn't.

This was a joke. But Dinah's mother didn't laugh.

After the abduction, after Dinah returned home from rehab, her mother's visits became more frequent. The drive from Birmingham to Ypsilanti was nearly forty miles but not a sufficient deterrent for the older woman who'd given up her volunteer work in Birmingham, she'd said, and her friends, to "help out" her "disabled" daughter.

Dinah had grown to dread the sound of her mother's voice as she knocked on the front door—"Dinah? I know you're home. Please open this door."

If Dinah wasn't feeling well, lying on a sofa in the living room, at the rear of the house, her mother was likely to come peer in the window, shading her eyes to make out Dinah cringing beneath a blanket.

"Dinah! Let me in, or I'll call 911. This isn't normal."

Sometimes, Dinah was lying on Robbie's little bed. In Robbie's room on the second floor.

This room had not been altered since the day of Robbie's disappearance of course. It was a small room beside Dinah and Whit's bedroom and when Dinah had been pregnant with Robbie she'd fantasized having a door between the rooms that might be kept open at night. Like a nursery in a fancier sort of house.

Now, the room was a small-boy's room. There was a four-foot bookcase Whit had built for Robbie out of glass blocks and in this bookcase were Robbie's storybooks—quite a few, in fact. In a paralysis of hope and dread Dinah would remove one of the books from its shelf—*The Littlest Fox,* with its astonishingly beautiful watercolor illustrations—and quickly skim the familiar text, that she and Robbie had both memorized. She recalled how, when she read the story to Robbie, he'd begun to read along with her, running his finger beneath the words. He'd gotten ahead of Mommy, sometimes! She could hear his voice, which left her shaken.

On the pale-blue walls of Robbie's room were more of the child's drawings and paintings as well as photographs and snapshots that Robbie, with his somewhat quirky taste, had particularly liked: some were pictures of himself, and Mommy and Daddy; one was Robbie with pre-school classmates at the Montessori school, and their smiling vivacious Miss Jameson; others were glossy pictures of animals—dinosaurs, a gigantic octopus, lions, elephants, giraffes, antelopes, wild horses. Recently Robbie had become fixated on horses and had it in his head that Mommy and Daddy should buy a farm in the country so that he could have a pony.

"And who would take care of the pony?"—Daddy had asked.

"Me."

"*You?* By yourself?"

"Well—me and Mommy."

They'd repeated this exchange many times. Why it was so funny, Dinah couldn't say. But they laughed, and laughed.

Well—me and Mommy.

More recently Robbie had taped to his walls posters of hulking figures dressed for intergalactic space, or for war—video-game-like warriors that were unsettling, in a child's room. Dinah had told Whit that she wasn't ready for this yet—Robbie was only five years old! Whit said, sensibly, We can't censor our kid. Don't even try.

Now that Robbie was gone, Dinah wondered if she should remove the warrior-posters? Reasoning that, when Robbie returned, he'd have forgotten them—wouldn't he?

Mid-mornings when Dinah's medication caused her to weave groggily along the upstairs hall it was natural to her to enter Robbie's room and lie down carefully—not fall down, limp and exhausted—onto the little bed which was always neatly made-up.

"Robbie. Oh, Robbie . . ."

She lay very still. Tears gathered in the corners of her eyes and spilled over onto her cheeks.

"It was my fault, honey. I should never—never—have let go of your hand."

She held her breath waiting for Robbie to speak to her. She did not exhale her breath for so long, her heart began to beat irregularly.

"Can you hear me, Robbie? It's Mommy. We're looking for you, honey, and we will never, never give up."

Dinah! Dinah!—there came an urgent rapping on the door downstairs.

The rapping was at the front door. If Dinah didn't hurry down to her mother, or had not the energy to hurry down to her mother, the rapping would recommence at the rear door.

Dinah! Are you in there? Where are you? Let me in.

Let me in, Dinah! Or I will call 911.

So Dinah had no choice but to hobble downstairs. To let the Fury in.

Wanting to say *You had your chance to be a good, loving mother and you weren't interested. Why now?*

Dinah's mother had many times apologized for being a "distracted" mother when Dinah had been a little girl. The fault had been primarily "your father—you know how he betrayed us."

Dinah's father had separated from her mother when Dinah was ten. Dinah's impression was that her mother had driven her father away and when he'd gone she'd laughed telling her friends—*Good riddance! He wasn't half a man, anyhow.*

As long as Geraldine had the house on Summit Drive, Birmingham. As long as Geraldine received monthly alimony and child support.

She'd never remarried. Possibly she'd never found a *whole man* who'd wanted to support her.

Since the abduction Dinah's mother had been interviewed on Ypsilanti–Ann Arbor TV and for the local newspapers. The "terrible anguish" of her beloved grandson being abducted "in broad daylight"—the "frustration" of waiting for law enforcement to find him—the "faith in God," that Robbie would certainly be found. Dinah read her mother's interviews in dread of what her mother might say impulsively—"My daughter did no wrong. She *did not let that child out of her sight for a minute*."

Whit read such interviews snorting in derision and tossing the paper down.

"Your mother is really getting off on this, isn't she! Like it's some kind of hobby for her, in her boring life."

"Whit! She's serious. She loves Robbie. This is very hard for her, too."

There was drama in Dinah's mother's life now. In her circle of friends—of whom most were divorcées like herself, or widows—it was Geraldine McCracken who was the center of attention, invariably.

She'd had her hair styled and lightened so that it shone now like a synthetic peach. She'd bought new clothes—in which to appear on a local afternoon TV talk show as *the grieving grandmother of missing five-year-old Robbie Whitcomb of Ypsilanti*.

For a week or ten days in late May, there'd been a distraction —Dinah's mother had discovered a cyst in one of her breasts, that had had to be removed for a biopsy; during this brief time, Dinah's mother had not visited the house on Seventh Street, nor had she called more than a few times. What relief!

The cyst had been benign. Dinah's mother returned.

Until finally Dinah told her mother please, she couldn't see her for a while.

"What do you mean, you 'can't see me for a while'? What kind of a thing to say is that, to a woman grieving for her lost grandson? Her only grandchild?"

"Mother, just go away."

"'Go away'—where?"

Dinah's mother had been too astonished to be angry. She'd thought it altogether natural, Dinah supposed, that, in her daughter and son-in-law's house, she had the right to answer the landline, and to speak knowledgeably to whoever was on the other end, in the matter of Robbie; she had the right to answer reporters' questions, and to be interviewed, without troubling to learn who a reporter was, and for what publication, if any, he was writing. She had the right, as Dinah overheard her saying, to proclaim *Both my daughter and son-in-law are devout Christians. We are praying for Robbie to be returned and he would be, if the police had more gumption to make arrests.*

"It's Whit who wants to send me away, isn't it? Your— 'husband.'"

Dinah's mother's lip curled, at the word *husband.*

"No, Mother. It isn't Whit, it's me. Please will you just *leave.*"

"You're sick. You're not in your right mind. You've taken too many pills. How can I leave you alone?"

"I have not taken 'too many pills'! I don't even take all the pills that are prescribed for me." Dinah tried to speak calmly. She was hearing Robbie in another room, chattering brightly. He had questions for her—she had to get to him, to hug him tight.

"I—I may have to report you, Dinah. I should call the medical clinic—your doctor—"

"Mother, go away! I'll call you when I want to see you again but it won't be for a while."

Now Dinah was speaking wildly. Far from being drugged she was cursed with a clarity of perception cruel and pitiless as a shining knife blade. She hid her ravaged face in her hands hoping that, when she lowered them, the Fury would have vanished.

Your "husband." Where is he?

Most days, all day into the evening Whit was at the radio station or—elsewhere.

Since the abduction he stopped by Ypsilanti police headquarters regularly, never less than twice a week. He'd taken an active role in the search for their son. He'd organized volunteers in the Ypsilanti–Ann Arbor area to search for Robbie and to affix MISSING CHILD posters in public places. He'd been many times interviewed on TV and radio and he'd traveled in Michigan, Ohio, Indiana, Minnesota to meet with law enforcement officers, city and state police, sheriffs' departments. He spoke regularly with FBI officers assigned to his case. The face of Whit Whitcomb—intense, pained, earnest—was nearly as familiar in the public gaze as the face of the lost child Robbie Whitcomb.

Whit Whitcomb had become a volunteer for the Missing Children of America Foundation and had several times been interviewed on national cable channels—CNN, MSNBC.

He continued with his popular WCYS-FM program. It had become a call-in program now, and many people called to commiserate over the DJ's abducted son.

He saw friends. Not friends whom Dinah knew but male friends, whom he'd known before his marriage. Sometimes, returning home, he smelled of alcohol.

Dinah thought *It's the smell of grief. Who can blame him.*

Her mother hinted, and more than hinted, that *a man like Whit Whitcomb* wouldn't be faithful to her for long. *A man like that, it's in the genes.*

What precisely did Dinah's mother mean? Whit's genetic pool was immense, you had to suppose—that was what *mixed-race* meant.

Pursue *race* far enough back, you'd probably end in an ancient kingdom somewhere in Africa.

Now that Dinah was *disabled.* Now that Dinah's face *needed more surgery.*

Her mother protested: she was just speaking frankly! She was just saying what everyone was thinking.

It was true, Whit was away from home on an average of twice as much as he'd been before the abduction. He often missed dinner, which he'd tried never to miss before. He never watched the TV channels he'd watched with Dinah and Robbie—Animal Planet, Discovery, Comedy Central; he never watched TV at all. When he was home, he was at his computer, scrolling the Internet. Checking e-mail obsessively.

Yet Whit called home faithfully, never less than once a day. He called Dinah's cell, not the special landline number.

Hi honey. How's it going?

Pretty good. You?

Great.

Any news?

I guess not. You?

Guess not.

A pause then. In the background, raised voices and maybe laughter. For Whit inhabited a bright peopled world from which Dinah was exiled for now.

Are you hurting, Dinah?

No! Not bad at all.

You had kind of a bad night last night—I guess?

Did I? No.

Maybe tonight will be better.

Maybe.

Well. Love you, Dinah.

Love you, Whit.

See you later.

How late?

Not past nine. Promise.

Whit didn't always keep his promises.

Dinah never reproached him. Lying on the sofa watching TV—not really watching, just clicking through channels as if in search of—what?—she didn't know—until midnight. She'd lost so much weight in the hospital and in rehab, she now ate frozen yogurt out of the container, ravenous with hunger, a kind of desperate greed, that ended in abrupt satiation, self-disgust. Then she'd drag herself upstairs to bed.

Thinking *He will never make love to me again. I am so broken.* Thinking *I would trade that—all that—for Robbie.*

Dinah's new friends were mostly women from the rehab clinic. Physical therapists, nurses, other patients. Rehab is a small closed world. You soon learn the language. Her physical therapist was a Jamaican woman named Rachelle whose fingers were soft, soothing, yet strong and deft. If Dinah broke down and cried, in pain and despair, Rachelle said *Now hon you don't mean that. You just get that out of your system, hon. Three minutes.*

If another patient stared at her raggedy face Dinah didn't shrink and hide behind her hands as she would have liked to do but smiled and struck up a conversation.

Hi! It's "reconstruction," I was in a pretty bad accident. I have one or maybe two more surgeries to go.

And: *It isn't as bad as it looks! I have my eyesight and great new teeth.*

Quickly the afflicted learns that affliction can be mined to some purpose. No one more popular than the cheerful-afflicted. Dinah had learned: misery does love company.

She spoke of Robbie, if she was asked. She spoke quietly and calmly and did not hesitate. She knew that, as everyone told her, as the police urged her, the more people who knew about her missing son, the more people who saw his picture, who were prompted to think about him, the more likely there might be a "lead."

That was how missing children were often found, police said. You wouldn't believe how accidental, sometimes.

Brightly she said *Yes. The search is continuing. This summer we will drive—around Michigan, we think. Just take the search into the rural counties. Of course the police and the FBI are on the case, they've promised to never let it rest.*

Her dark desperate moods of wanting-to-die she hid. Her frantic moods of screaming-for-Robbie she hid. She could muffle her crazed mouth in a towel, if necessary. She could cry, cry, cry until her eyes flamed and swelled and her tear ducts were emptied like her heart and not even Whit would know.

Whit snoring in their bed. Dinah crouched in the bathroom sobbing into a towel.

Seeing, God!—even her toenails looked misshapen, growing in sideways. Everything about her broken and askew except her knife-sharp memory of the child's fingers wrenched from hers.

She knew he was alive. She knew he was yearning for her. Yearning for her and his daddy. Wherever he was, she knew.

How did she know with such certainty, *she just knew.*

In this way, and in other ways, they waited.

12

KITTATINNY FALLS, NEW JERSEY JULY, AUGUST 2006

Gideon? Come here, son.

On hesitant bare feet the child came.

The child's rapt staring terrified eyes.

The child in pajama bottoms.

The child's little chest showing milky-pale skin pulled tight against his ribs.

Climb onto Daddy's lap, Gideon. C'mon!

In a trance the child did not move.

I'm commanding you, Gideon: climb onto Daddy's lap.

They were in the TV den, as Daddy Love called it.

A leather sofa, a single chair. Rattan rug. A thirty-inch TV. In a window, a rattling air conditioner in the humid midsummer heat of New Jersey. Over both windows, heavy damask curtains as well as black blinds.

It was cuddle-time. It was bedtime.

It was *that time*.

* * *

Darlene? Hi.

It was OK now, he thought. He could call the woman, and have her do some cleaning. She could meet Gideon.

The kid was so quiet, might've been deaf-and-dumb. No danger he'd begin babbling or crying to Darlene Barnhauser who was a stranger to him.

Come over to the house, can you? When's a good time?

You can meet my little boy Gideon.

Yeah he's here with me, the rest of the summer. I drove out to Traverse City to get him.

Darlene said some wiseass thing about the boy's mother, some cunt-wisecrack, Chet Cash laughed like kicking sand.

Yeah. Somethin like that, Darlene. But we don't talk about her here, OK? Not ever.

Darlene said, more sober, I got it, Chet.

Sooner or later you require a female, it was a fact. Certain kinds of things like scrubbing, scouring with Brillo pads, airing out bedclothes on a clothesline, mopping the linoleum floor in the kitchen—it was female scut-work and if you weren't married to the female, or sleeping with her, you'd have to pay.

Chet resented it. But hell, Darlene was OK. Poor whites in this part of rural New Jersey, like in the Ozarks, Appalachia. Little wood-frame houses, trailer villages. Darlene smiled her brave lipstick-smile and you saw that half her teeth were discolored and one tooth missing.

It made him laugh, the female was in love with *him*.

He had that power over women—Chet Cash.

His swaggering walk, his hair tied back in a ponytail. T-shirts showing his lean-muscled chest, jeans low-slung on his hips. A zipper glinting at his groin.

He'd washed the face-powder out of his beard. Now it was mahogany-dark again, bristling and virile.

In the run-down area of Kittatinny Falls, Chet Cash was a property owner.

He'd inherited the old farmhouse, falling-down outbuildings and forty acres of farmland on the Saw Mill Road from a woman he'd met in the Church of Abiding Hope in Trenton, New Jersey, in the 1990s. The sixty-nine-year-old widow had had adult children who'd "abandoned" her, as Chet Cash, in his late twenties and early thirties at the time, would not. Mrs. Myrna Helmerich was her name. And, for a while, before she'd died of heart failure, in her tidy little brick house in Trenton, in 1999, Mrs. Chester Cash.

It had been Chet Cash's sole marriage. Except for the minister who'd married them, no one knew.

It had been a legitimate marriage, in the Church of Abiding Hope on South Washington Street, Trenton. The Reverend Thornton Silk officiating.

The woman who'd been a widow for eighteen years became a wife again at sixty-nine. Her ponytailed bearded hippie bridegroom had been thirty-one. They were both devout Christians in the Church of Abiding Hope which was a multiracial church. Myrna Helmerich had been a volunteer in the

Presidential-candidacy campaign of Eugene McCarthy in 1968 and she'd been active in civil rights organizations in the 1970s. Her wedding dress was white muslin and braided into her silvery-white hair, that fell loose to her shoulders, were lilies of the valley. So fey and otherworldly the bride looked, you expected to see that she was barefoot but she wore white ballerina flats. Chet Cash wore a sharp-looking cranberry-velvet suit with a vest, acquired from a veterans' secondhand clothing shop in Trenton. He'd trimmed his beard and secured his ponytail with glittery silver twine. To the married couple, age was not an issue. Myrna was given to gaily saying *You are as young as you feel!* Chet Cash was given to saying *Myrna is my heart and soul.*

Under New Jersey law, property in the possession of one spouse becomes the property of the other, in the eventuality of the spouse's death. To insure this, the Cashes drew up their wills.

In addition, each was insured for fifty thousand dollars—this was Chet Cash's idea, to which Myrna Helmerich deferred.

In addition to Myrna's property in Grindell Park, Trenton, there was a farm near the Delaware Water Gap, of which Myrna spoke negligently, for she hadn't visited the property in years, and had only a vague idea of what condition it might be in.

In the little stucco church on Washington Street, in which the couple first met, Chester Cash had been a member of the choir and a volunteer for youth counseling, as Mrs. Helmerich had been the choir leader and a volunteer for youth and "single mother" counseling. Chet Cash was a gregarious and popular presence in the Trenton church and soon he'd been invited to serve with the Mayor's Community Outreach Program, that had received a one-million-dollar funding from the State of New Jersey.

Soon then, Chet Cash was in charge of financial accounts for the Outreach Program. He'd met the mayor, Leander Hollis, who'd taken a liking to him, as a *white dude* who could make you laugh. Chet Cash was making deposits, making out checks. Chet Cash liked to say *In the right place at the right time. That's what we mean by destiny.*

A photograph of Chet Cash and Mayor Hollis shaking hands and smiling at the camera had been framed and hung on the wall first in Myrna Helmerich's Trenton house, then in Myrna Helmerich's Kittatinny house, which Chet Cash inherited. Both men were handsome: Chet Cash resembled a shaggy Brad Pitt (so admirers said) and Leander Hollis resembled ex-heavyweight champion George Foreman. Chet was disappointed that his friendship with the popular Democratic politician had seemed to fade and woke sometimes in the night wondering *Why?*

He hoped it wasn't a race thing. He'd thought that Hollis was above that kind of primitive thinking.

Daddy Love's son at the time had been Deuteronomy. The less said of Deuteronomy's final years, the better. The sandy-haired boy was sulky and pimply-faced by eleven, fattish, lethargic, and suffered from chronic constipation, eating junk food with Daddy Love and watching TV seven nights of the week. And when he didn't watch *Texas Rangers, Cops, Law & Order, X-Files, Superstars of Wrestling* with Daddy Love, he played video games—just the same three or four, repeatedly, that Daddy Love had bought him. Deuteronomy didn't attend school: the vague theory was, Chet Cash was homeschooling his son. The mother had died, somehow—fast-acting cancer. This was a story told to whoever expressed any mild curiosity, but few of their neighbors did. Father and son lived upstairs in a brownstone duplex on Trotter Street which intersected with State Street a mile from the gleaming-white dome of the New Jersey State capitol building. Nearby too were the New Jersey State Court and the Mercer County Court in a run-down neighborhood of pawnshops and bail bondsmen.

Deuteronomy didn't yearn to get out much, any longer. Downtown Trenton was "shitty" in his opinion. He'd "run away" more than once, but had always returned to Daddy Love by suppertime. The kid had no friends—of course. His friends were TV-figures, video-game-figures whom he routinely slaughtered, or was slaughtered by. Like a captive dog chained in a basement for too long he'd lost his appetite for out-of-doors. If he remembered his old family, in some hick town in eastern Ohio, he never let on. Daddy Love thought the kid's brain was probably a *tabula rasa*—a fancy term for a blank slate on which you could write anything you wanted, if you wanted.

Deuteronomy did cry, sometimes. A wet-blubbery noise, in the bathroom.

In Daddy Love's bed the boy was limp and unresisting. He'd learned not to resist but had never learned to (voluntarily) kiss Daddy Love, not anywhere on Daddy Love's body. He'd never so much as *touched* Daddy Love unless commanded.

The kid's penis resembled a skinned baby rabbit, that rarely got hard. Daddy Love hadn't been excited by it in years.

Daddy Love felt sorry for the kid, he'd lost his looks by age ten. There wasn't much point in keeping him but his daddy was feeling the kind of dumb sentiment you feel for an elderly blind and incontinent dog—you can't kill the mutt but you wouldn't mind if somebody else ran him over in the street for you.

Mrs. Helmerich, who'd become Mrs. Chet Cash in January 1998, was never to meet Daddy Love's son. She was never to hear the name Deuteronomy.

Nor did Deuteronomy know about Mrs. Helmerich. If he had, Daddy Love knew that the boy would have been wildly jealous.

But soon after Mrs. Helmerich came into Chet Cash's life, Deuteronomy departed.

This won't hurt, son. It's B-12 vitamin for quick energy and a kind of a diet pill, you've been growing a gut, eh!

In Kittatinny Falls it was Chet's account that he'd bought the Helmerich farm, as it was locally called. It was to be a *spiritual retreat*. In the countryside north of Kittatinny Falls, the property was still called the Helmerich farm even by local residents like Darlene Barnhauser who knew Chet Cash was now the property owner.

Steady, kid. She's nobody you know.

The child so flinched, Daddy Love had to hold his skinny arm firm.

The child was staring mesmerized seeing Darlene Barnhauser striding in their direction. Daddy Love had tried to prepare the kid, he'd be seeing a "friend"—Daddy Love was well aware, this was the first person the child had seen since the Ypsilanti mall four months before.

Except for TV-people. Daddy Love did not forbid TV.

The Barnhauser female, nothing like the kid's scrawny mother. Yet, the way the kid was staring at her, twitching and trembling, Daddy Love had to wonder if he wasn't confused thinking this *was* his mother—not the way he remembered her, exactly.

Green-parrot T-shirt showcasing her large saggy breasts, short-shorts showing too much of her lardy veined thighs, and flip-flops on her pudgy feet. Her hair was stacked atop her head gypsy-style and her wide mouth was greasy-red.

Ohhh God, Darlene said, her eyes swimming, i'n't he *cute*.

My little boy Gideon, Chet said proudly. He's come to live with me, maybe more than just this summer.

"Gideon"?—that's a real nice name. Hiya, "Gideon"!

Chet Cash squatted beside the boy, gripping the skinny arm. It was fascinating to Daddy Love, how the child gaped up at the Barnhauser female as if—what?—his five-year-old brain was trying to connect her with someone else.

The child was trembling. Shivering. Daddy Love felt rather than heard his teeth chattering.

The temperature had been in the low nineties through that day.

Chet Cash said, Looks like me in the eyes and around the mouth, don't he? That's what people say.

He does. Oh God, Chet, i'n't he *cute*.

His name is Gideon. "God's warrior."

He's kinda shy, huh? Not like his daddy.

Darlene was squatting too in front of the child. Couldn't resist touching his curly-kinky hair as the boy stood stiff and unmoving staring at her and his watery eyes now rapidly blinking.

Daddy Love had dyed the boy's hair. No longer was it so dark as to appear black but a dirty-blond color, like a ravaged beach.

The previous night, the boy had had to be disciplined. First, Daddy Love filled the sink with cold water and commanded the boy to lower his face to it, and when the boy resisted, Daddy Love seized him by the neck and forced his face into the water counting *One two three four five*.

Then, he'd spent the night in the Wooden Maiden and not in Daddy Love's bed. A sponge-gag in his mouth and rags stuffed around his ass, to soak up urine.

Daddy Love felt sorry for his son, almost. But discipline comes first, in training.

Daddy Love didn't let Gideon out of the Maiden until around noon by which time the little boy was weak, famished, so ravenously hungry that he gobbled his food like an animal, and began to puke.

There were several punishments for puking. Daddy Love had tried them all.

Gideon, son, say h'lo to Darlene. She's our friend and neighbor, see? She's come over to help us. And maybe if your daddy has to travel somewheres, Darlene will look after you.

Ohhh—I'd love that. He's so *cute.*

The child's little finger had healed, that had been broken through the child's carelessness. Daddy Love hoped that Darlene wouldn't notice the bone had healed at a slight, stiff angle from his hand.

Darlene was cooing to him. Whyn't you say h'lo to me? Sweetie?

The child's chocolate-dark eyes with their thick lashes did not seem to be entirely in focus. As if Darlene loomed so large before him, his eyes could not absorb her.

Daddy Love was wondering if Darlene thought there might be something wrong with his son. Retarded, or maybe "autistic" —you heard a lot about that, these days.

Tell Darlene where you come from, son.

Daddy Love gave the boy a little shake. He was gripping his arm tight, which had to hurt, but the boy was learning not to wince or whimper.

Hey? Tell Darlene where you're from.

The boy's lips moved but his words were inaudible. The boy was still staring and blinking at busty Darlene as if—(was this it?)—he was hoping she'd turn into someone else, who had come for him.

At last like a windup doll Gideon began to speak.

From T'vers Cit-ee, Mich'gan.

What's that, sweetie?

He says—"From Traverse City, Michigan." Where his mother lives.

Ohhh! That's a long way.

Tell Darlene how we came here, son.

In a stammering voice the child said they'd come by a "special box."

Chet laughed irritably, and gave the kid another little shake.

He means, in my van.

(Since he'd come to Kittatinny Falls, Chet had removed the eye-catching white cross from the roof of the van, and he'd spray-painted the van another time, now dark red. The patina of paints suggested something rippling beneath the surface but Chet thought the Chrysler looked pretty good considering its age.)

Tell Darlene about your mother, Gideon.

Now the child began to speak more rapidly. These were prepared words, that sprang from his lips with ease.

Bad Mommy. She *smoked*.

Darlene laughed. Well, Gideon—lots of mommies do. We're not perfect.

Bad Mommy. She *smoked*.

The child repeated his few words. He smiled—a quick eager smile. Chet was stroking his arm, twining his fingers around the child's small fingers.

Darlene said, Oh—Chet. Gideon has wet himself, I'm afraid.

Chet shrank away. Chet was repelled.

Pissed his pants! God-damn baby.

Chet was embarrassed as well as angry. Darlene intervened, taking Gideon by the hand. I'll mop him up and change him, Chet. No problem.

God-damn *baby*. Five years old, you'd think his drunk-bitch-mother would've housebroke him by now.

This was a joke and so Darlene laughed, though not with much mirth. Clearly she was concerned for the frightened little boy, who was gripping her hand, tight.

I'll clean you up, hon, and change you into some clean clothes. Don't mind your daddy, it's how men are. They take some things too serious, and other things not serious enough.

Daddy Love followed Darlene and his son into the house, to the downstairs bathroom. Beyond was Daddy Love's bedroom that was surprisingly neat, for one of Gideon's household tasks was to make Daddy Love's bed every morning and to pick up his scattered underwear and socks and place them in a rattan basket in a corner of the room.

It was Daddy Love's practice to remove the Wooden Maiden from this room and to keep it in a closet, in case of a chance intrusion like this.

He'd been using the Wooden Maiden less frequently, now Gideon was becoming trained. Sometimes the boy was shut into the Maiden but the mask was left open so he could breathe better and could see—if just the ceiling of the bedroom.

Tonight? Daddy Love hadn't decided.

Darlene ran water, in the bathroom. When she began to pull down the boy's shorts, Gideon pushed at her hands with a whimpering sound.

Gideon! You let Darlene take care of you. She's a real nice lady willing to clean you up decently—so let her.

The child ceased resisting. Darlene pulled down his shorts, and his little white undershorts that were damp with urine. Fastidious Daddy Love backed off a little, into the hall outside the bathroom, but he didn't go away, he dared not relax his vigilance.

Hearing Darlene murmur to the boy, cooing and laughing. There was no doubt of it, a female had a way about her, a certain generosity, kindness. A female naturally took to young children, it was her instinct. You could ask a female to do almost anything and she'd do it—if she liked you. If she thought there was a chance you might like her.

Here was a secret: Gideon was *on trial*.

Every day and every hour. Every night.

Cuddle-time at night was the test. Too often, Gideon failed the test.

Crying, and resisting, So Daddy Love had no choice but to use *brute force*.

(Which was exciting to Daddy Love, in fact. For Daddy Love was contemptuous of weak, puling, unresisting boys.)

(Still, Daddy Love could not allow rebellious behavior in any son of his, and the son so *young*.)

After Daddy Love disciplined the boy in his bed, careful to place a bath towel on the bottom sheet beforehand, and a sponge-gag in the boy's mouth, and wiping away, afterward, blood from the boy's skinny haunches, it was necessary to force the boy into the Wooden Maiden for an undetermined period of time.

You will learn, son. Disobeying Daddy Love leads to one thing only.

And if you persevere, you will pay with your life.

Comprenez?

Through the summer, through the months of the boy's *trial,* it was not always clear how Daddy Love felt.

Sometimes, Daddy Love was crazy about the boy.

His eyes just feasted on the boy.

He felt that stirring—the sex-stirring, unmistakable.

Recalling how by the bunny enclosure in the mall the beautiful little curly-black-haired boy had glanced up at Daddy Love and with the slyest of smiles poked his pink little tongue between his lips . . . And the look that passed between them, the mother oblivious, a look of utter secrecy, a scorching look—*I don't want to be with her, I want to be with you. Take me with you!*

But other times, Daddy Love wasn't so sure. The boy was so quiet, you'd be inclined to think that he was simple-minded, but Daddy Love knew this wasn't the case, it was a pretense.

He'd seen Gideon stealthily looking through things Daddy Love had brought into the house—local newspapers, the Trenton *Times,* a magazine called *New Jersey Sportsman.*

(Could Gideon read? He didn't seem capable of reading but he did stare at columns of print and sometimes his lips moved, silently.)

(It would be Chet Cash's claim that his son was *mentally disabled* and so would not be starting school for a while, if ever.

No one had ever challenged Chet's prior claims, for Nostradamus, Deuteronomy, or Prince-of-Peace, each of whom had been
mentally disabled.)

Hey, son: c'mere.

Upsie-daisy! C'mere.

They would watch *Friday Night Raw: Wide World of Wrestling*.

They would share a cheese-and-pepperoni pizza, a big bottle of
Diet Coke, a container of blackberry-ripple Turkey Farm ice cream.

Gideon was shy and wary when Daddy Love summoned him,
after Daddy Love had disciplined him. But then, when Daddy
Love was sincerely loving, the boy responded with relief and grati-
tude like a dog that has been kicked but is now petted and loved.

The boy responded by eating slices of pizza held in Daddy
Love's hand. Hungrily eating, choking and coughing, but eating
in a way to please Daddy Love.

Food is love, son. Who loves you, feeds you.

Who feeds you, loves you. *Comprenez?*

With the passage of time, Daddy Love boldly experimented with
taking the boy into the *outside world*.

Little Gideon didn't resemble his old, Ypsilanti self much.
Daddy Love didn't think so. The influence of Daddy Love was
such, the boy had grown to resemble *him*.

And there was the dirty-blond hair.

And a new look in the boy's eyes—no longer *young*.

This eerie sensation Daddy Love felt, like injecting crystal
meth into a vein, when he drove the boy into Kittatinny Falls,

or down to Lambertville, New Hope—walking hand in hand with Gideon into the Safeway, or the drugstore, or the hardware store, or the lumberyard—walking with his little boy like any father, with the quiet pride of a father. *See? I'm a normal guy. This is my little guy.*

And sometimes—(the sensation of risk and elation was almost unbearable)—Daddy Love would strike up a casual conversation with another father in the company of a son, for instance at a Little League softball game. Is one of them your son?—so Daddy Love might ask.

The young father would point out his son. The scrawniest homeliest kid, yet the father would be proud of him. Friendly Daddy Love would ask how old his son Gideon had to be, to try out for the Little League, though he knew the answer already, so he and the other guy get to talking, and maybe—(this happened more than once)—he and Gideon would be invited to a barbecue that weekend.

July Fourth, they'd been invited to two barbecues. In Kittatinny Falls and Lambertville, New Jersey.

A frank-faced friendly attractive man looking no older than thirty-two or -three, with a child gripping his hand—other fathers naturally liked you, and females were all over you.

I'n't he *cute.*

He's takin after his daddy, for sure.

What's your name? "Gid-eon"?

How old's he?

Where y'all livin?

This went well. This was exciting! Daddy Love loved seeing himself and his son through others' eyes.

There was the thrill deep in Daddy Love's gut—how audacious he was. How daring.

Law enforcement officers would be astonished. *He'd brought the abducted boy with him, in public places. In plain sight.*

Once, Daddy Love braked his van to a stop at the side of the River Road, to hike back to where a Lenape County sheriff's deputy had parked his cruiser behind a stand of trees, lying in wait for speeders. Daddy Love had his son with him in the van, buckled into a child's seat in the rear.

Excuse me, officer? Can you tell me—where is the Water Gap post office?

The cop told Daddy Love to keep driving. A few miles ahead, he couldn't miss it.

Thanks, officer! I appreciate it.

He'd confronted law enforcement officers, with the abducted boy in his van!

In public, in the presence of strangers, Gideon was very shy and quiet; other children his age babbled and jabbered happily, but not Daddy Love's son.

His eyes darted quickly about, however. You could sense—(Daddy Love could sense)—that the five-year-old was excited and stimulated and calculating, though he rarely spoke, and rarely smiled even when strangers smiled at him.

(Daddy Love had warned the boy countless times: call attention to himself or in any way embarrassing or upsetting Daddy

Love, he'd be *waterboarded* in the sink, locked in the Wooden Maiden and left to suffocate in his own shit. And that was if Daddy Love was feeling merciful.)

(They'd played the Game of Strangle a few times, earlier in the summer. Daddy Love had said, This game is not to punish you, son. You have done nothing wrong and merit no punishment. This game is just to warn you what an appropriate punishment might be if you did do wrong.)

Many times the child had been instructed: his old life was *dead and gone*. His parents had given him up for adoption because he was costing them too much money so, might as well think of them as *dead and gone* too.

There's many thousands of orphans, son. Like shelter animals. They're kicked out by their parents, and their lifetime in the shelter is limited. D'you know what *euthanasia* is, son?

Meekly Gideon shook his head, *no*.

Euthanasia is when a living thing is killed because nobody gives a damn for it. Nobody loves it.

Meekly Gideon stared at Daddy Love's feet.

For often, Daddy Love did not want Gideon to look into his face but only at his feet in a posture of abject submission.

Euthanasia is what happens to approximately forty percent of orphans, whose parents have gotten rid of them and who nobody else wants to adopt. You're God-damned lucky—Daddy Love chose *you*.

Meekly Gideon stared at Daddy Love's feet. His eyes swam with tears.

Say it: "I am a very lucky boy."

Gideon's lips moved: *I am a very lucky boy.*

Louder, son. And like you mean it: "I am a very lucky boy."

Again, in a near-inaudible voice: *I am a very lucky boy.*

Like your life depends upon it, son: "I am a very lucky boy."

Daddy Love's voice had grown louder. A vein throbbed in Daddy Love's forehead.

At last Gideon spoke audibly: *I am a very lucky boy.*

It was how you trained any animal, Daddy Love knew. By repetition, reinforcement. By rewards and punishments. In the special case of Daddy Love's son(s), unpredictable rewards and punishments were recommended.

Like the Game of Strangle. If Daddy Love was bored and listless, this would turn him on, fast. But if Daddy Love was in a mellow mood, the Game of Strangle could turn into the Game of Tickle and the boy would be encouraged to laugh.

The point was, never to let the kid take you for granted.

Never to let the kid take his life, his very breathing, for granted.

Yet, Gideon must trust Daddy Love, as a loving child would trust his loving father.

You know that I love you, son? Right?

Yes.

You *know* this—right?

Yes, Daddy.

And you trust me, right?

Yes.

Trust me with your life, right?

Y-yes. Daddy.

Sometimes Daddy Love strung the boy up—skinny wrists bound with twine and tied to a spike high overhead in Daddy Love's bedroom. So tight, the child had to rise onto his toes, which made his little chest swell out, oddly—the rib cage prominent inside the milky-pale skin.

The sponge-gag in the child's mouth, so that he couldn't whimper, whine, cry or scream.

A partly clad little boy. Bare on top but his small bottom covered with (torn) shorts. The nakedness of the child was apparent through the (torn) shorts.

Daddy Love sprawled on his bed, observing.

It was an unfailing turn-on. Sure thing, Daddy Love was never *bored*.

Daddy Love cared for the boy, in fact: made sure that the twine didn't cut into the boy's wrists, by wrapping gauze around the wrists first. A boy so beautiful, you don't want to scar him.

He will know by such ways, you care for him.

And he will be grateful.

13

Gideon. These knots are *wrong*.

Daddy Love was instructing the child in the art of macramé.

At the Gift Basket in New Hope, Pennsylvania, fifty miles downriver, where Chet Cash had struck up a friendship with the divorcée proprietor, macraméd purses, tote bags, belts, dog-sweaters, wall-hangings were displayed, and sold to tourists at remarkably high prices.

Chet Cash had introduced himself to Edwinna Oldman as an *artist*.

Mostly a painter/sculptor—but lately he'd been seeing the artistic possibilities of macramé.

Proudly he'd introduced his little boy, too—the woman with the penciled eyebrows and blue plastic eyeglasses squatted down, with a cheerful little grunt, to shake his hand.

Why h'lo, Gideon!

Friendly Chet Cash had so *suaved* this female, she'd pressed her card upon him, invited him and his son (of course) to have supper with her in her "river place" in New Hope and Chet Cash said maybe sometime soon but he was caught up in work now, macramé wall-hangings were his specialty.

So, it had happened that the Gift Basket would be an outlet for the child's macramé efforts, if the child would only learn.

It ain't hard, son It's some kind of female scut-work you do with your fingers, like knitting. You learn the basic steps and just keep repeating with some little changes, and changes in color. See?

He'd seen some scribble-drawings the child had done, on paper bags from the Safeway. The child had some small talent, possibly. Daddy Love's first thought was *My son could be precocious! What's it called—prodigy.*

Daddy Love bought Gideon Crayolas, colored chalks, a child's watercolor set. But the child hadn't seemed inspired, with Daddy Love watching him.

(Gideon preferred scribbling on paper bags, and hiding these from Daddy Love. But you could hide nothing from Daddy Love.)

The macramé was more practical, with an outlet for their products more or less promised at the Gift Basket—if Gideon could learn the basic skills.

He was a smart kid. He was learning by his mistakes.

Daddy Love remembered to praise the boy when Gideon did something halfway right. That was the Skinner-method of conditioning: praise not blame, rewards not punishments. But hell, punishments were *fun*.

Also, only just rewards would give Gideon a false sense of the world which is a harsh place, not a kindergarten.

There was something to say for the Preacher promising Hell for sinners and for the enemies of Christ. A congregation had the right to expect Heaven for themselves and Hell for *those others*. A smart man-of-God gave his congregation what they needed.

Fucking macramé knots were maybe harder than they looked. Daddy Love was having a hell of a time. The kid's fingers were small, though—that should help.

Wall-hangings were the easiest, you could more or less copy designs from the Internet, with some small changes each time. Nobody who bought macramé hangings in New Hope, Pennsylvania, had the right to expect original works of art. The purses and tote bags were more complicated but you could charge more.

Try these knots again, son.

The child tried. But fumbled, failed.

Keep trying, son. *I'm warning you.*

This went on. Hours.

Daddy Love went away, and when Daddy Love came back the kid had made only a little progress.

Patient Daddy Love said, That's better, son. Just persevere.

By the end of the day, the child had created a twelve-inch strip of not-fucked-up macramé—a vivid bright green. Son, this is promising! This is a very good start, son.

Shyly Gideon smiled.

Tomorrow, you'll do better. And you'll do more.

Shyly Gideon smiled. A weak hopeful yearning sort of smile.

We'll be in business together, eh? *Cash & Son.* Maybe open our own store, with a studio people can visit.

But later that day, at suppertime, the child was vacant-eyed and failed to smile when Daddy Love spoke to him in a kindly manner. It infuriated Daddy Love to think that at such times the child might be thinking of his *old life.*

Running his fingers through the child's curly hair—(that needed dyeing again, soon: the dark roots were showing)—Daddy Love did not like it that the child flinched just slightly. And his left eyelid twitched.

Not afraid of your daddy, are you, son? Your Daddy Love?

N-no, Daddy.

Now both the child's eyelids twitched. His little face strained and unsmiling.

D'you mean to piss off your Daddy Love? This some kind of *mutiny*?

His son was reminding Daddy Love of his former son(s) who'd disappointed him, and infuriated him.

Daddy Love's fingers twitched. Daddy Love was a *hands-on* kind of daddy.

I'm asking you son—is this some kind of—*mutiny*?

Quickly Gideon shook his head, *no.*

Whatever *mutiny* meant, Gideon knew the answer had better be *no.*

But Gideon was skittish now. Nervous as a kicked dog.

Fumbled a soup bowl from the microwave and it fell to the floor—gave a little scream, the liquid scalded his hands—and Daddy Love was on him with a curse punching and kicking, in disgust. And cleaning the floor with the scrub mop, the child was trying not to cry, sulky-faced, unmistakably Daddy Love recognized the sulky face of rebellion, waited until the boy finished with the floor then hauled him into the bedroom by the nape of his neck, threw him down on the floor and dragged the Wooden Maiden out of the closet, that he hadn't used for a while—(Christ, that was the problem: he was getting soft on the kid, the kid was taking Daddy Love for granted)—and tried to force his son into the Wooden Maiden, but the boy was fighting back, crazed and screeching, like a wildcat clawing and biting and Daddy Love slammed him down onto the floor, tore off his soup-stained clothes, "disciplined" him right there on the floor thump-thump-thumping his small body against the floor until the kid was semiconscious and bleeding from the ass and it was no trouble then forcing him into the Wooden Maiden and slamming both lids shut, and locking them.

Except he'd forgotten the sponge-gag. And the diaper.

Telling himself *If he screams, he will never be released.*

That night, Daddy Love slept in his bed. And Gideon his son, in the Wooden Maiden a few feet away, was very still.

If he's dead in the night, tough shit. Daddy Love has zero tolerance for wiseguys.

And in the morning, Daddy Love ignored the child. A single kick to the Wooden Maiden, to wake the kid up if he was still asleep, to let him know it was fucking morning and daylight and Daddy Love went away and didn't return until noon at which time he had a sudden rush of tender-heartedness, took pity on the boy, unlocked the face-mask, and the lower lid, and there was Gideon seemingly part-conscious, sickly-white in the face, and traces of vomit on his chin. A harsh smell of urine wafted from the Wooden Maiden.

Daddy Love kicked the Wooden Maiden another time, to rouse the boy.

Jesus! Get out of there. You ain't dead and you need to clean yourself up.

You got work to do—*chores*. Plus the fucking macramé.

Stand up! Stand yourself up. You are capable of *standing up*.

The child's eyelids fluttered. The child was panting—weirdly, since he hadn't been exerting himself for twelve hours or more.

The child made a motion, to sit up—but sank back down as if exhausted.

We've got work to do, son. We ain't gonna laze around all day even if it's summer. C'mon, get up.

Still the child was too weak to sit up, still less to lift himself from the casket-like container.

Lay there in your own shit, then! Fucking baby.

Daddy Love walked out in disgust and slammed the door.

Half-hour later Daddy Love happened to be on his cell phone talking with Pastor Silk at the Church of Abiding Hope in Trenton, arranging for a Sunday soon in October when the Preacher would preach to the congregation, when he saw, outside the window, the little half-naked boy running and stumbling from the house in the direction of the old falling-down hay barn.

Jesus!

Daddy Love let the little phone fall to the floor. Daddy Love ran out of the house and after the child who must have slipped from the house by the back door—intent upon escape.

Not to the road. Not yet.

Hiding in the barn—was that it?

A scuffling movement, a sound—from a storage shed, beside the barn.

This was a rat-infested structure, near as Daddy Love could figure it had been a storage place for rusted old tractors, old tires, and corncobs. Maybe the corncobs had been fed to cows, years ago?

Gideon? Where are you?

He wasn't inside the shed. Daddy Love knelt to peer beneath the shed, into a space so narrow you couldn't believe that anything could crawl there, let alone a five-year-old boy.

Gideon! Son! Come out of there.

Daddy Love was panting, and very hot. Daddy Love was shocked, *his son had tried to escape from him.*

He'd been certain of the boy's love. Their cuddle-times together were very sweet, usually.

He'd eaten from Daddy Love's hand enough times to know to trust Daddy Love.

He called to the boy. Cajoled and threatened. Counted to three slowly enough to give the boy a chance to obey—but the boy did not obey.

Fucking little brat. Don't you know, I could kill you?

Break your skinny little rat-neck. *Nigger.*

In his fury Daddy Love uttered words he didn't mean. For Daddy Love was not a racist.

Grunting Daddy Love lay on the ground on his belly to peer beneath the shed and could barely make out the child a few yards away. Come out, God damn you! I'm your father. You will obey me.

The child was very silent. Very still.

Daddy Love picked himself up, and went to the other side of the shed, to lie down again, panting, to peer beneath. You really would not have thought that any creature larger than a cat could squeeze into the tight space.

Know what, son? I'm going to burn this thing down. You got a count of three to get out, before you're burnt alive.

Again, Daddy Love counted slowly to three. But the child, in a paralysis of terror, did not budge.

Finally, Daddy Love staggered to his feet. He had no choice.

(Not fire. Daddy Love wasn't imprudent enough to set a fire on his property, and draw attention to himself and his domestic arrangements.)

Instead, Daddy Love ran to fetch his twenty-two-caliber rifle, locked away in a box beneath his bed.

There were other firearms in this box, which the child had never seen.

Like an infantryman trotting with his weapon, Daddy Love returned to the storage shed beneath which his mutinous son was hiding from him. He lay down on his belly and poked the barrel beneath the floor of the shed, pushing aside weeds.

You little nigger ingrate, you're in God's hands now. He is summoning you.

The first shot was a deafening *crack*. Even Daddy Love wasn't prepared. And the rifle had a considerable kick, he'd forgotten.

Now the child was whimpering and whining. Had he been wounded? Daddy Love had aimed to miss, but might have hit the kid anyway.

If it was a hit, and a severe wound he couldn't bind up, he'd have to let the kid bleed to death. No way Daddy Love was taking the kid to a hospital.

But the child didn't appear to be wounded. He'd crawled into another corner beneath the shed, behind one of the concrete blocks that held the rotted structure in place. Twisted in there, he was barely visible to Daddy Love.

Think I can't see you? Fucking little rat-nigger.

Daddy Love aimed again. Daddy Love pulled the trigger.

The child was crying in terror. But it was too late.

In all, Daddy Love fired five shots. Each was measured and deliberate. He shot to the right of the huddled child, and to the left of the huddled child. He shot in front of the huddled child.

Then, Daddy Love heaved himself to his feet. His ears were ringing from the damned shots. He went into the kitchen to fetch a cold beer and returned dragging a rusted lawn chair through the grass. Sat, and waited.

The other sons had died in Daddy Love's arms. He'd had his reasons for sending them to God for judgment, mostly he'd been pissed by adolescent insolence, and bored, and turned off by acne, but he'd made sure that they had died peacefully in his arms, and hadn't known a thing of what was happening, dumb-ass kids. This one, Gideon, the *mixed-race* son, was sharper-witted, you could tell.

Daddy Love held the rifle balanced on his knees. Daddy Love was undecided whether he'd kill the kid, when the kid crawled out. That was up to God. Like tossing dice.

After about twenty minutes, Daddy Love had a glimpse of something moving beneath the shed. The sun had shifted in the sky to afternoon. It was a humid-hot August day in New Jersey. Daddy Love smiled to see the boy's little head appear from beneath the shed like the head of a baby being born. There was magic in this! Daddy Love had summoned the child to return to him, to obey him, and the child was complying.

With difficulty the child dragged himself out from beneath the shed. He was covered in dirt. Seeing Daddy Love in the lawn chair about twelve feet away, he began to crawl toward him like a broken little animal.

It was the most beautiful sight.

Daddy Love had forgotten entirely about the rifle. He'd dropped the can of beer. Fell to his knees on the gnarly ground gathering the weeping child in his arms and tears streamed down both their faces like liquid sunshine.

"Son."

14

Dinah? Where are you, honey?

He'd returned home late. So far as Dinah could know it wasn't Whit's fault, he'd had to retape his entire program for that night which was factually true. Not his fault but he was feeling guilty, anxious. And Dinah wasn't downstairs though both the living room and kitchen lights were on. And Dinah wasn't in their bedroom which was darkened.

In Robbie's room, darkened also—there was Dinah lying on the child-sized bed, in her bathrobe, and barefoot—not responding when Whit called to her from the doorway, or leaned over her to shake her.

Dinah? Dinah? *Dinah?*

II

APRIL, MAY 2012

1

KITTATINNY FALLS, NEW JERSEY APRIL 2012

Strange!

Very strange striking sci-fi/fantasy images.

Probably he'd gotten them from TV or the Internet. Or maybe, video games.

What was the TV series—*Game of Thrones?* Maybe he'd been influenced by that.

It was hard to know if the boy was "talented"—or if he was (probably) just reproducing images. None of the teachers at West Lenape Elementary School was very familiar with the TV programs or video games favored by the older boys.

The sixth-grader's drawings and watercolors were finely detailed, with a look of the subterranean. A figure—(a boy?)—in a shadowy place—and a rectangle of light—(a window?)—that opened onto what appeared to be houses at a distance.

There were two distinct regions in the drawings: the shadowy space in which the figure dwelled, in the foreground, and a seemingly distant sunlit space outside a rectangular window.

In some of the drawings, the figure was lying in a casket(?) —with an opening at the top of the casket, so that the boy's eyes could be seen, widened and white-rimmed.

His body was hidden inside the casket, trapped. You had to imagine his arms straight against his sides. Trapped.

In some of the watercolors, which were more brightly colored than the drawings, and less ominous, the boy was in a canoe-shaped vessel that floated above the earth. All about him, stars and moons in a nighttime sky.

Inside the canoe-like vessel with the boy was an animal resembling a dog. Sandy-colored, with erect ears and a long curved furry tail.

A friendly animal! This was a relief. This was in contrast to the sinister tone of the drawings.

There were no art classes for students at West Lenape Elementary School as there were no music classes, for the public-schools budget had been severely slashed; but one of the younger faculty members, an English teacher with a certificate in art education, volunteered to teach art during study periods to interested students.

One of these interested students was Gideon Cash, a sixth-grader.

The teacher, Ms. Swale, was surprised by the boy's intensity, as by his strange, unchild-like talent. He'd been eager to draw and paint in a corner of the study hall but showed her his drawings and paintings reluctantly. He'd seemed to be discomforted by her praise.

It was a challenge to cajole him into lifting his eyes to her face. *He has this wounded look. But stubborn too.*

One of Gideon's most remarkable drawings, Ms. Swale told the other teachers, certainly had been copied from a painting by Goya—*Saturn Devouring His Children*. The boy's dark, finely shaded and cross-hatched drawing depicted a cruelly smiling bald-headed ogre about to bite off the head of a very small, doll-sized child whom he held in his fist as you might hold a peeled banana.

The art teacher said it couldn't have been a coincidence—it had to be "copying."

But you couldn't accuse an eleven-year-old of copying someone else's work.

Saying with a shudder, "That hideous cannibal-image can't be *original*."

Gideon Cash was a *shy boy*. So rarely spoke in class, you'd think he was *mute*.

Maybe, *deaf-mute*.

The father himself had suggested that Gideon was (possibly) "autistic"—to a degree.

Or, suffering from "Asperger's syndrome."

Even when his work was praised the boy stood silent, down-looking. His head appeared large for his thin shoulders and spindly lower body. His skin was putty-colored. A tiny fishhook-scar glinted just above his left eyebrow.

Did you hurt yourself?—Ms. Swale asked. That looks like a nasty little cut.

Gideon Cash nodded, *yes*. He'd hurt himself.

Gideon had begun school late, his father said. When he'd been a little boy and having health problems they'd been living in a rural community in Maine where the nearest medical clinic was thirty miles away and in the public schools there were no classes for "special" students.

His mother had died when Gideon was five, Chet Cash said.

Lung cancer metastasizing to pancreatic cancer. Six months from diagnosis to death.

Gideon never really recovered from losing her.

Neither did he.

So Chet Cash said, wiping at his eyes.

Then, they'd moved to New Jersey. Chet had tried to home-school the boy for a while but by the age of eight it seemed that Gideon might be mature enough to enroll in a school with "special" classes.

At the elementary school in Kittatinny Falls, Gideon Cash had surprised his teachers by learning quickly. He'd already known how to read, and how to do simple arithmetic; his father had suggested starting him in a class for learning-disabled students, but he'd been soon promoted to third grade.

It was true, Gideon Cash's "social skills" were undeveloped. He was both intensely aware of his surroundings and yet oblivious to them, as if he believed himself invisible. He shrank from his classmates. He seemed incapable of having a "conversation" with any adult—he could only listen, with a tremulous intensity, and a tense, nervous smile, and stammer an inaudible reply. He seemed to have difficulty hearing, or processing what he'd heard; when his teacher asked a question of the class, no matter in a friendly and smiling way, Gideon froze, in a panic that the question was addressed to *him*.

Teachers learned to speak softly to Gideon, as to a frightened animal, and to speak in a soothing, repetitive manner, to allow the boy to understand that there was no threat to him, and that the situation wasn't urgent.

Other children waved their hands excitedly, to answer the teacher's question. Gideon blinked and stared at the floor, twisting his fingers in his lap.

Rarely did Gideon smile. Never did Gideon laugh.

Alone among his classmates he never seemed to "get" any humorous remark. The boy, small for his age, only just sat at his desk frowning, staring and blinking like one confronted with a foreign language.

Yet, Gideon Cash's teachers said of him that they'd never seen any child so *eager to please*.

At first, in the Lenape grade school, Gideon Cash had virtually no friends. By fifth and sixth grades, he'd made a few friends among classmates shy and socially awkward as himself. He'd liked to linger in his homeroom volunteering for tasks like watering the teacher's numerous plants on a windowsill, or rearranging and improving the bulletin board. His teachers noted that he had something of the sense of responsibility of a much older child—an adult, even. He couldn't engage with

his teachers in anything resembling a normal conversation—
he rarely lifted his eyes to their faces—but he was touchingly
eager to be of use.

Remarkably mature for his age.

Intelligent, though lacking in self-confidence. Inclined to be anxious, though extremely well organized.

Sweet boy. But something wounded in him . . .

The loss of the mother, they supposed. The "sudden death" of the mother when the boy was so young.

Chet Cash, widower-father, brought the child to school most days in his cranberry-red minivan and picked him up after school as he didn't trust, he said, the school bus.

Maybe when Gideon was a little older. Maybe then he could ride the bus with the other children.

His son had a delicate soul, Chet Cash said. He had to be protected against older, rougher children.

Chet Cash was an aggressively friendly man who might have been in his late thirties or early forties. He had a swaggering air. His thick dark hair he wore loose to his shoulders, like the boy general Custer in a TV epic, or tied back in a rakish pigtail, like a TV drug dealer. He exuded an air of the *special, unique. Unclassifiable.* His flat gray eyes were sharp, keenly alert even as he joked and laughed. When he visited the school to speak with his son's teachers, which he did at least twice a year, he wore a white cotton shirt, or a flannel plaid shirt, with a necktie, he wore laundered jeans, or khakis. He wore hiking boots. He expressed an air of parental concern for his son who was, as he said, *a very special boy* and his *only living heir*. But when his teachers praised Gideon, Chet Cash frowned as if doubtful.

"Gideon is a good boy. He's been trained to be good. I guess I didn't realize how 'smart' he is—he hides that, around the house—but I know how *good* he is."

And he said: "It's a welcome thing to hear that Gideon is smart, too. I thank you."

Though he lived in the countryside south of Kittatinny Falls, approximately seventy miles from Trenton, it was rumored of Chet Cash that he was an ordained minister in a Trenton church. He didn't appear to be a full-time minister and he'd listed, when filling out forms for the Lenape County school district, his occupation as *farmer & artist.*

It was known that Chet and his son lived on the old Helmerich farm on the Saw Mill Road, that hadn't been a working farm for twenty years. Affably he complained that they grew just a few "crops"—barely for themselves—and harvested what they could from the old apple orchard.

His primary source of income, Chet Cash said, was the sale of his "artworks"—mostly, macramé products supplied to outlets in the Delaware Valley.

There didn't appear to be any woman in Chet's life at the present time.

Gideon's (female) teachers were impressed by Chet Cash. A widower-father, he was obviously a very attentive father; you could see how he loved his son, and was protective of him, by the way he held the boy's hand at a school open house, for instance, and absentmindedly cupped his hand around the boy's head, as he spoke with Gideon's teachers.

Chet Cash hadn't seen his son's drawings and paintings until the April PTA open house. Ms. Swale would report to her colleagues that Gideon's father had been visibly *surprised.*

"Such striking images, Mr. Cash! Your son has quite an imagination."

The father was staring at drawings of shadowy, confined figures gazing with widened glassy eyes at windows flooded with light, and airy watercolors of child-figures borne aloft in a nighttime sky.

"My son did *these?*"

"They're remarkably skillful for an eleven-year-old. Or—for anyone, of any age."

Beside Chet Cash stood the eleven-year-old Gideon, stiff, stricken with shyness, eyes cast down. He was wearing jeans and a plaid flannel shirt that fitted him loosely, as if it were a size or two too large for him. Very still and stiff the child stood as the adults discussed the drawings and paintings posted on the classroom wall and his father stroked his hair, and the nape of his slender neck.

"You can see how different Gideon's 'art' is from the other children's. There's an actual technique he's used, in the cross-hatching. It's hard to believe he's only a *child.*"

"Yes, ma'am," Chet Cash said slowly, "my son has quite an imagination."

"He's gifted, Mr. Cash. He should be encouraged. Even if—possibly—he has copied some of these images from the Internet."

"Yes. 'Monkey-see, monkey-do.' But my son isn't allowed access to the Internet, ma'am, or video games. Only TV which he watches with adult supervision."

Ms. Swale hadn't put up the drawing of the bald-headed ogre about to bite off the head of a miniature child. *That* she'd hidden away in a drawer.

Other parents with their children intervened. Chet Cash moved among them, pleasantly smiling, in the direction of the classroom door. Beside him his son moved haltingly, guided by Chet Cash's grip at the nape of his neck.

"Mr. Cash? Wait . . ."

The art teacher hurried breathless after the father and son to ask if they were leaving already, before the reception?

Chet Cash said pleasantly he regretted having to leave. But he had work to do, and Gideon had his chores.

"Maybe—sometime soon—you'd like to come to my house for dinner? I live in town, just a few blocks away."

Chet Cash smiled deeply. A smile that didn't lift into his stone-colored eyes.

"Why thanks, Ms. Swale. That's very thoughtful of you."

"Please call me 'Brittany'—Chet."

"'Brittany.'"

Yet Chet Cash scarcely paused, moving in the direction of the classroom door, his hand at the nape of the child's neck.

* * *

In the van they rode silently out to the Saw Mill Road.

The child was gripping his hands tight in his lap. The child was having difficulty separating his thoughts from a powerful roaring in his ears.

Now it will happen. You knew it would happen.

The child understood that Daddy Love was both angry and "calm"—the "calm" of Daddy Love when he was very, very angry.

The child had in his hands a thick brush he'd found in the storage shed, much thicker than a common paintbrush, possibly a brush used for some particular purpose around the old farm, like spreading tar, and this brush he'd dipped into something black, yes it was tar, hot steaming tar, and he was spreading the tar across the road in front of the van so that the van would careen into it . . .

The hot black tar was ▆▆▆▆ so thick no oxygen could penetrate it.

Trying to drive the van, trying to breathe, Daddy Love grew faint and lost consciousness and the van veered off the road and downhill rapidly in the direction of the Delaware River . . .

"Son?"—Daddy Love's voice was startling-close.

Son murmured *yes Daddy.*

"Your teachers are impressed with you, they say. Your daddy is proud of you."

Son murmured *yes Daddy.*

It was a familiar landscape through which they drove. Returning to the farm on the Saw Mill Road. Yet, it was a strange landscape, without color.

The hot tar had vanished. But the hot tar had taken all the colors with it like it's said there is no color in anything at the time of a lunar eclipse.

To the right was the Delaware River, a dull muddy-gray like dirty pavement only just visible through the trees. To the left, abandoned and overgrown farmland.

It was early spring. Most of the trees were still leafless, but beginning to bud. This was a *special time* of year, he knew. Daddy Love said it was his birthday, in April.

He was eleven years old, Daddy Love said. Daddy Love had showed him his birth certificate with a gilt-gold seal from the State of Maine, Hecate County.

He'd been born, this document declared, on April 11, 2002. His parents were *Ceila Cash* and *Chester Cash*.

Daddy Love seemed proud of this document. He'd had several printed up, for safekeeping.

"You don't remember your mother, Gideon. She was a lousy mother blowing *smoke* into a baby's face."

He'd known better than to ask where his mother was. For Daddy Love was in charge of all such information, to be doled out when Daddy Love wished.

"In fact your mother died a horrible death, of cancer, from smoking."

"In fact your mother died a *deserved death*. From her habit of smoking."

Yet, Daddy Love had sometimes said that Gideon's mother was living in the north of Michigan. He'd looked up Michigan in a book of maps at school and saw the *Upper Peninsula*—"Traverse City."

The surprising thing was, Daddy Love himself sometimes smoked. Daddy Love kept packs of cigarettes in secret places in the van and in the house. In the *safety-box,* as Daddy Love referred to the long wooden box in which Gideon was sometimes locked, for reasons of discipline, Gideon could smell the smoke from Daddy Love's cigarette two rooms away, even if the face-lid was shut.

There was the terror, that the face-lid would never be opened. The *safety-box* would never be opened.

But always, the *safety-box* was opened eventually—by Daddy Love.

Smiling Daddy Love, lifting Son to his feet.

And how Son loved Daddy Love, at that moment! There was no love so powerful.

It was a *special time* of the calendar now. It was *April.*

Gideon had worn only a light jacket to school that day. But a wintry chill had descended from the overcast sky like broken concrete.

Daddy Love turned the van off the River Road, and onto the Saw Mill Road. They were less than two miles from home.

Quick before he could think how dangerous such a move might be if it failed Gideon seized the steering wheel and turned it as far to the right as he could and Daddy Love was too surprised to steer the van back onto the road and the van went thump-thump-thumping across the ground dropping down to the river . . .

The van would sink. The doors could not be forced open, because of the water pressure. Muddy water would seep into the van, slowly at first and then more rapidly. It was a scene you saw on TV. It was a familiar scene. Yet, no one would rescue them for this was not TV. The daddy would not be able to force the door open and "rescue" the son for this was not TV.

Daddy Love's hair which was dyed-dark hair would lift, in the water, like snake-tendrils. Daddy Love's eyes crazed in fury and the curses in his mouth drowned in the muddy water, and then silent.

What happened to Son wasn't clear. It was only Daddy Love who mattered.

Son did not seize the steering wheel. In a paralysis of inaction Son remained hunched in the passenger's seat beside Daddy Love gripping his icy-cold fingers in his lap.

And there was the wood-frame two-story farmhouse Son had helped Daddy Love (partly) repaint the previous year, a startling robin's-egg-blue—"Son. We are home."

2

KITTATINNY FALLS, NEW JERSEY APRIL 2012

The eager young dog Missy, Daddy Love had allowed his son to choose, for his tenth birthday the previous year.

A surprise, Son.

For you've been a good son.

And your daddy loves you *a lot.*

D'you know what *grace* is?—being loved way beyond what you deserve. *God's grace.*

In the Lenape County Animal Shelter. He'd been so excited about the prospect of a dog, his eyes had welled with tears. Silly, he'd been trembling!

Daddy Love close beside him. Daddy Love's hand heavy and firm on his shoulder.

A windowless room of animals in cages. Dogs, puppies. There was an excited yipping in the room, he didn't know where to look first.

A smell of animal-urine, animal-anxiety.

Almost he was feeling faint. Almost he was feeling he'd have to run outside for if he was sick to his stomach Daddy Love would be very upset with him.

Yet, Daddy Love guided Son along. Past the cages which were stacked one on top of another, three cages high.

A cage of cocker spaniel puppies . . .

A cage containing a single, older splotched-coat dog with rheumy eyes and a tail that lay unmoving . . .

A cage containing a small terrier-like dog on his feet, barking, and his tail wagging frantically . . .

A cage containing more puppies, and a skinny and exhausted-looking mother, of some mixed-breed Labrador retriever and beagle . . .

A cage containing a German shepherd, youngish, with anxious eyes and a slow-beating tail . . .

A cage containing a sand-colored long-haired young dog with alert eyes, pricked-up ears, a sharp-beating tail . . .

As Father and Son walked along the row of cages, a din of barks, yips, whines assailed their ears.

Two categories of dog, Son observed.

Those who were yearning to be taken home by strangers, loved and protected and brought into a family, and so they were on their feet amid a cacophony of barking, tails wagging and whipping—*Me! Me! Take me!*

And those older dogs who'd given up.

A clutch of terror came into Gideon's throat. For even the older dogs who lay unmoving in their cages were looking at *him*.

Daddy Love was talking with the shelter attendant. Asking questions about the dogs, their ages, breeds. Daddy Love said he and his son were looking for a dog already trained and house-broken and a work-dog, a reliable guard-dog, not a *lazy useless dog*.

Daddy Love said they wanted a dog that barked when there was a reason for barking, for instance an intruder on their property, but otherwise didn't bark, and certainly didn't *yip*.

Gideon knew the dog he wanted. Almost immediately he'd known.

The sand-colored long-haired dog, a mix of border collie and golden retriever, that had leapt to its feet and was eagerly pressing against the cage bars as Daddy Love and Gideon paused in front of the cage.

The dog's eyes swimming with anxiety, yearning.

Take me! Take me with you!

Already I love you! I would die for you.

Daddy Love insisted upon considering all the mature dogs. Gideon waited scarcely daring to breathe to see if Daddy Love would allow him to choose as he'd promised.

Father and Son. Chet Cash and his ten-year-old, fifth-grade son Gideon. The animal shelter attendant would note how close the two were, how the father seemed protective of the son, touching him, letting his hand fall onto his shoulder.

Finally, Daddy Love said to Gideon, with a shrewd Daddy-wink: It's this one you want, eh? But she's a female.

Gideon hadn't known that. *Female.*

The attendant said, Yes. But Missy has been spayed and has all her shots and her former owner only gave her up because he'd gotten sick and had to move in with some relatives . . . A very sweet affectionate gentle dog looking for a home.

Anxious Gideon said *Yes.* This was the dog he wanted.

Daddy Love poked his fingers into the cage. At once the sand-colored dog licked Daddy Love's fingers, eager and grateful. Her tail thumped wildly.

Daddy Love said, What's her name?

The attendant said, *Missy.*

As Daddy Love parked the van in the driveway, there came Missy trotting toward them eagerly, tail thumping.

To the jarring end of the chain-leash that Daddy Love used to "secure" Missy when he and Gideon were away from the house.

Missy knew not to bark, for Daddy Love had many times disciplined her.

"Dog"—so Daddy Love called her.

Gideon called her "Missy." Gideon loved loved *loved* Missy.

Missy was Gideon's responsibility, utterly. Gideon fed her twice daily and kept her plastic food-dishes clean. He kept her water-dishes filled with fresh water. He brushed her coat, which was a warm beautiful sand-colored coat that tended to snarl, with a special dog-brush. Especially, Gideon was zealous about keeping her from barking at the wrong time.

Except if someone turned into the cinder driveway or came uninvited to the front door of the house. Then, Daddy Love liked "Dog" to bark loudly.

And Daddy Love approved of "Dog" chasing rats. Chasing away raccoons and woodchucks and rabbits, that made their way into the fenced-off garden behind the house, where in summers Daddy Love and Gideon grew tomatoes, melons, sweet corn, peppers.

Gideon knew: it was not good to fasten a chain-leash to a dog's neck for the dog's neck soon becomes tender and develops bleeding sores. But Gideon knew better than to say anything to Daddy Love who could not be criticized or questioned in any way.

Mutiny, such questioning was. An expression in Son's face, a narrowing of Son's eyes, might qualify as *mutiny.* And so Son learned to keep his expression neutral and his eyes downcast.

Sometimes, Daddy Love was annoyed—and then angry—if Son indicated, for instance, a preference for pizza with cheese and tomatoes and not pizza with cheese, tomatoes, and pepperoni sausage which was their customary pizza; or a Big Mac without melted cheese; or a TV program that conflicted with Daddy Love's favored programs.

Mutiny was (maybe) a joke. For Daddy Love often joked.

Yet, Daddy Love's jokes were serious. As a young child, Son had learned that Daddy was most serious often when he was smiling and joking. You could not predict Daddy Love's *true meaning.*

It was unpredictable each night: whether Daddy Love would allow "Dog" to sleep in Gideon's room.

It was unpredictable: whether Daddy Love would bring Son to sleep with him in his room.

(But lately, since Gideon's tenth birthday, Daddy Love didn't bring Gideon to his bedroom so much as he had previously. Or, sometimes, bringing Gideon to his bed, having had several beers Daddy Love just fell asleep, and snored, his heavy hairy leg thrown over Son's naked body. Nor did Daddy Love find the need to discipline Son by locking him in the *safety-box* as much as he once had.)

By the time Daddy Love parked the van in the driveway Gideon was so anxious he could barely open the passenger's door and half-climb, half-fall out.

Thinking *Why! Why did you do it.*

He felt a stab of fury against Ms. Swale.

It was wrong to blame Ms. Swale for what had been his own fault, yet Gideon blamed her.

Running to Missy and kneeling as Missy licked his face with her soft damp coolish tongue.

Hiding his face in Missy's neck. Hugging Missy tight.

The sensation of excitement tinged with dread, dread tinged with excitement, that had begun in the school was increasing. Almost, Gideon couldn't catch his breath.

Daddy Love stood a few yards away, contemplating. For his visit to Son's school he'd worn fresh-laundered khakis, his single white cotton long-sleeved shirt, and a polka dot bow tie his woman friend at the Gift Basket had given him. He'd shaken hands with Son's teachers and a few other parents, concerned daddies like himself. But now he was home, and the bow tie came off in his disdainful fingers, and was thrust into his pocket.

"You, Gideon. You and 'Dog.' You two have something to account for."

Son didn't hear this. The roaring in his ears was such, only Missy's quickened breathing and the beat of her heart were audible to him.

Daddy Love strode into the house. Gideon was unleashing Missy, since they were home now, and Missy wasn't likely to run away.

Distinctly if faintly Gideon heard: the sound of the refrigerator door opening, and shutting.

(Was this a good sign? Or—not-so-good?)

(One beer, Daddy Love was in a mellow mood. Several beers, Daddy Love was in a judgmental mood.)

Gideon called Missy to feed her, on the back porch. Eagerly Missy nudged against his hands, and began eating kibble.

And still, Daddy Love did not reappear.

It will be all right Son was thinking.

Squatting beside Missy. Petting her thick hair, her smooth head.

All right. It will be. Missy is not to blame.

Gideon was thinking it had been risky, to love the adopted dog. In the animal shelter, risky to have locked eyes with any of the dogs. There was a curse on Daddy Love's son, that could spill over onto anyone or anything that came too close to Son.

Then, suddenly, Daddy Love did appear, on the back porch. Daddy Love with the twenty-two-caliber rifle slung over his shoulder.

"Stand aside, Son."

Frowning Daddy Love lifted the rifle and pointed the barrel at Missy who glanced up from her food bowl, ears pricked to attention.

"Daddy, no!"—the words were torn from Son's throat. And desperately Son knelt in front of the dog.

"Get out of the way, Son. I'm counting to three."

Son was sobbing, clutching at Missy's neck. The dog was upset, and had overturned her water bowl. Her tail was frantically thumping and she began barking at Daddy Love.

"You know, Daddy Love has forbidden a *barking dog*."

Daddy Love circled the boy and the dog, sighting along the rifle. Daddy Love's face was ruddy and his stony eyes shone.

In opposition, Daddy Love found great joy. You would not ever want to come between Daddy Love and great joy.

The rifle fired—but the shot missed. Missy leapt away, and Gideon lost his balance and fell to the ground.

"Daddy, no! *No!*"

The panicked dog didn't seem to know whether to flee for her life, or to protect her young master. She was barking loudly, as

Gideon had not ever heard her bark before, and she was barking
at Daddy Love as he aimed the rifle at her chest, while Gideon
crawled on hands and knees daring to tackle his father's legs and
pitch him off balance.

Daddy Love cursed—"God damn you to hell, nigra."

The rifle discharged another time. The bullet went wild.

"Run, Missy! Run! Go away!"—Gideon shouted, clapping
his hands at the dog even as Daddy Love regained his balance,
and brought the stock of the rifle down hard against Gideon's
head, knocking him flat against the ground and unconscious.

When he woke, in the dirt, it was late afternoon.

His head pounded with pain. Blood had trickled from a cut
in his scalp, wetting the dried earth.

At first, he didn't remember what had happened. He had no
idea where he was.

Then, he remembered. In panic he pushed himself to his hands
and knees, looking for Missy—but she was nowhere in sight.

He saw, though, blood-drops in the dirt. A scattering of bright
red splotches leading in the direction of the storage shed, and
beneath its rotted floor.

Plaintively, weakly he called—"Missy!"

3

KITTATINNY FALLS, NEW JERSEY APRIL 2012

Bicycled into town.

One Saturday morning when Daddy Love had taken the van to deliver macramé products to his "retailers" in the Delaware Valley.

For Daddy Love did not forbid Son bicycling a few miles provided Son did not *interact with strangers.*

In Daddy Love's vocabulary, all persons—including even Son's sixth-grade classmates—were *strangers.*

Son had no plan. Gideon had (maybe) a plan.

Son lived in present-tense. Son was *is.*

Gideon lived in past-tense. Gideon was *was.*

Except, Gideon was smarter than Son. Gideon was older than Son and so could live in present-tense if he wished, and in future-tense.

Son had smothered in the *safety-box.* Son had not survived.

Son *had* survived. But as a worm survives making itself small, twisted, flat.

Son was not Gideon.

Son said to Daddy Love *Yes Daddy. I love you Daddy.*

Gideon said to Daddy Love *Yes Daddy.* But thinking his own (mutinous) thoughts.

Son had wept seeing Missy beneath the storage shed floor, unmoving.

Called to her and saw her tail thumping—once, twice . . .

Son had cried helplessly. Gideon had wiped his eyes and the blood from his dirty face and crawled under the shed, to bring Missy back out.

Two bullets had entered Missy's chest. The beautiful fur suffused with white but now stained with blood.

Furious Daddy Love gave the order: bury it.

It! Gideon would never concede, even in death Missy was *it.*

In his (mutinous) thoughts Gideon loved Missy more than he loved Daddy Love though Missy was no longer breathing and no longer *alive.*

Oh but it was so hard to believe—hard to comprehend . . . That Missy was no longer *alive.*

She would never lie in the bed he'd made for her of old towels and blankets, at the foot of his bed. She would never lie in Gideon's bed pressing her warm head against his thigh through the blanket on those nights when Daddy Love had no use for Son.

He'd thought that Missy might still be alive, when he reached her. But he'd been mistaken.

He'd been breathing strangely. Like running, you can't catch your breath. He'd felt blood drain from his face. He'd tried to pick up Missy but her body was heavy, uncooperative.

"Fucking nigra. You will learn."

Daddy Love was disgusted with Gideon. Daddy Love had struck Gideon on the side of the head and knocked him unconscious and later when he saw the weeping boy crawling from beneath the shed pulling the lifeless dog with him he'd strode to Gideon and gave him a good hard kick in the chest.

"Drag it! Drag it and fucking bury it and get it out of my sight."

Son had obeyed. Son never failed to obey.

Gideon's hands blistered digging Missy's grave.

Out behind the garden he dug the grave. So that Missy could see the apple orchard which would soon be coming into blossom and was a beautiful hue of rosy-pink-red among the new green leaves.

Missy had loved to romp out of doors. Running with Gideon in the orchard, in the fields behind the barns. Chasing scuttling creatures—mice, rats?—in the old hay barn.

After Missy was buried and a small rock placed to commemorate her grave Daddy Love hauled Gideon into the house to further discipline him in the *safety-box* which was almost too cramped for Gideon now, he was eleven years old and tall for his age.

"I should dump this in the river. See how far it floats. Only Daddy Love's mercy will save you."

Gideon, covered in bruises and welts.

Gideon, whose hair required dyeing now in the spring of 2012 but Daddy Love was too disgusted to take the time and so chopped and struck at the boy's hair with a scissors, then carelessly shaved his head with a razor, so the boy was stubble-headed, freaky.

At school, all would stare at him. *Freaky Gideon Cash!*

His classmates were becoming wary of him, however. No longer was he shy Gideon Cash with downcast eyes but in recent weeks his eyes were uplifted, glaring.

It was late in the month, nearly three weeks after the PTA class day.

Gideon, who'd refused to change his clothes for gym class saying his daddy had told him *No nakedness.*

They'd been astonished at West Lenape Elementary. What was this—*nakedness?* The boys were never naked but always clothed.

Public schools no longer required showers for students, following gym classes. No one was *naked.*

Gideon said his daddy had said if anyone looked upon his *nakedness* there would be a lawsuit—"Big time."

So, Gideon hadn't had to change his clothes for gym class. He'd been allowed to spend gym-class time in the library which was one of his favorite places.

No one had seen Gideon's bruises and welts that were beneath his clothes. The bruise and cut on the side of his head he'd explained—carefully, as Daddy Love had instructed him—was the result of falling from his bicycle on the Saw Mill Road, bicycling into a pothole.

His homeroom teacher was concerned saying that the cut on his face should be looked-at by a doctor and might require stitches and to this Gideon had no reply for Gideon hadn't seemed to hear.

Daddy Love had threatened to remove Son from school if his teachers were too inquisitive. He'd homeschooled him once and could homeschool him again.

For Chet Cash had taken courses at Wayne County Community College, in Detroit.

In the youth facility at Traverse City he'd taken several courses and his teachers had praised him.

Damned bad luck, I never had a scholarship to go to a hoity-toity college like Harvard, Yale. Fuckers never gave me a chance.

Saturday mornings Daddy Love took the van to deliver macramé products—brightly colored wall-hangings, belts, purses, tote bags, plant hangers, chair seats—to his *retailers*.

These were women who owned gift shops in Lambertville, New Jersey, and across the river in Pennsylvania in the tourist towns of New Hope, Washington Crossing, Center Bridge, and Raven Rock.

The labels on the macramé products stated FROM THE STUDIO OF CHET CASH, KITTATINNY FALLS N.J.

The women praised Chet, warmly. Seems like women were Chet Cash's closest friends.

Really good work, Chet! Very nice.

Our customers don't want "original"—this is what they want.

Maybe more of the smaller purses? We can retail them for fifty dollars.

And plant hangers. This is the season!
Gideon had been making macramé things since—so long!—
he couldn't remember what he'd begun. Of course Daddy Love
supplied the materials and directed him—each week Daddy
Love had orders from his "retailers" to fill.

Doing macramé knots was easy for Gideon now. Like most
of his household chores macramé was an opportunity for him
to split his brain off from his hands and think his own thoughts.
Quick deft skilled hands, a child's hands. But growing.
As Gideon was growing.

Liking the quiet-time when Daddy Love wasn't hovering
over him or talk-talk-talking to him about life, death, good,
evil, God and Satan and Fate and he could direct his thoughts
elsewhere.

Trying to remember, for instance, the beginning of the macramé
—and what had come before the macramé.

He'd had another daddy then—had he? And a mommy who'd
cuddled with him but not like Daddy Love cuddled with him . . .

She'd held his hand, tight. They'd been walking in a big space
like a parking lot. She'd been scolding him—maybe. Daddy Love
said that his parents had "sold" him to an adoption ring and that
he, Daddy Love, had "rescued" him the way you might rescue
a doomed animal from animal shelters.

And if you rescued the animal, the animal was no longer
doomed.

Daddy Love had said *You owe your life to Daddy Love. Every
breath you breathe.*

Another thing Gideon remembered. Riding on his bicycle along the Saw Hill Road and to the River Road, suddenly he remembered.

Like a lump of something undigested, rising into your mouth. An ugly taste to make you choke.

Daddy Love and Son watching nighttime TV. Years ago when Son had been *little*.

Eating just half of a Big Mac, a few French fries and sugary coleslaw and Coke out of Daddy Love's bottle. And Son was secured in the crook of Daddy Love's arm the way on TV wrestling a wrestler was secured by another, stronger wrestler. Except this was *cuddle-time*. And there were two TV-people talking about a boy who'd been *abducted* four years before in the Midwest and the boy had just been found by police only sixty miles from his home and returned to his family at the age of fifteen and the abductor was arrested and the subject of the discussion was *Why hadn't the boy left his abductor for he'd had plenty of opportunities it seemed: his abductor had taken him out in public and neighbors saw him often believing he was the abductor's son for the two seemed to get along well, in public at least;* and the talk-show host who was a favorite of Daddy Love's had said, in a disdainful voice, *Looks to me like the kid could've gotten away lots of times. Looks to me like he'd come to like his new life better than with his old family—no school, hanging out, skateboarding, eating pizzas . . . I'm suspicious of this kind of thing, kids running away from home and claiming to be "victims."*

Daddy Love laughed excitedly for Daddy Love revered the sarcastic talk-show host and had several times sent the man e-mails praising him. It was Daddy Love's hope that he might someday be interviewed on the cable channel talk-show and his "true story" be aired to the American public.

Looks to me like the kid was getting along pretty well with his "abductor." There's more here than meets the eye and the "liberal media"—you can quote me.

Son had been very sleepy after his heavy greasy/sugary meal and soon fell asleep in the crook of Daddy Love's arm.

Bicycling two and a half miles into town.

His backpack strapped to his back.

At the outskirts of Kittatinny Falls was the First Methodist Church where sometimes Chet Cash and his son attended Sunday morning or Wednesday evening services. And there was the Kittatinny Falls Volunteer Fire Co., where Chet Cash and his son visited when there were tables set up in the driveway at Memorial Day, Fourth of July and Labor Day and food was sold that had been prepared by the firefighters' wives and you could mingle with the firemen and shake their hands and talk with them as Chet Cash did, and buy a casserole or two, loaves of bread, cookies and cakes. (Many young kids at the firemen's open houses as they were called, many young parents like Daddy Love with whom he could talk in his open frank friendly way.) And there were the houses—large, wood-frame Victorians, attractive and relatively opulent homes built above the Delaware River

decades ago for owners of the mills downriver at Lambertville
—where Chet Cash shoveled snow after a sudden snowfall, a
volunteer snow-shoveler, with his young son at his side; for the
houses were likely to be owned by elderly individuals, or women
living alone. (So Chet had determined. A week in a new place,
Chet knew an astonishing amount about his neighbors through
what he called *firsthand observation*.)

It was a curious thing to do, shoveling front walks and driveways for strangers. But Chet Cash wasn't bound by conventional
behavior—not Chet! He explained that he'd been brought up
to "help" where "help" was needed, and not to wait to be asked.
And if the homeowners had arranged for their driveways and
walks to be professionally plowed—that didn't matter.

Shoveling snow is great exercise, Chet Cash said. It's like
singing—God suffuses your body at such times. You feel *good*.
Helping neighbors is always *good*.

Chet Cash and his little boy Gideon were invited into each
of the houses. Indeed there were elderly residents in the old
Victorian houses and among them two widows living alone in
households built for large families. They were touched by Chet's
kindness and solicitude and insisted upon feeding him and the
quiet little boy.

What's your name, son?

"Gideon"—that's a nice name.

And how old are you, Gideon?

Raising a son is a challenge, Chet Cash said. Especially alone.

There were women who could help him, Chet Cash was told.

He knew. He understood. But his memory of the boy's mother was so powerful in his heart, he wasn't yet ready to see other women except as friends.

The boy isn't ready for a substitute mother, just yet. The boy is still in mourning.

In town, Gideon bicycled past West Lenape Elementary on Spruce Street. Bicycled to the intersection with Church Street, and turned right, ascending a hill behind the lumberyard. Ms. Swale's house was on Church Street, he knew: the address was sixty-seven.

Behind Ms. Swale's dull-brick house was an alley. Gideon turned into the alley but had difficulty riding his bicycle here for the ground was rutted and muddy.

He left his bicycle hidden behind a pile of debris.

It was late morning. There were children playing in fenced-off yards but no one was in the alley.

Most of the houses had garages, at the rear of their properties, abutting the alley. These were old garages, for the houses were old. There were broken windows, missing windows. There were rear doors that were unlocked or had never been locked and if you wished you could push one of these doors open and step inside quickly, and no one would have seen.

Kittatinny Falls was a small community, population 645 people at the last census in 2005. It was not a community where people locked their garage doors and often even their house doors went unlocked.

A beautiful blessed place to bring up a child. The cities are finished—God has departed from our cities.

In the alley he determined which house was Ms. Swale's. Which garage.

He'd heard—like Daddy Love, Gideon had a way of acquiring information without seeming to be acquiring it—that Ms. Swale lived with her mother and another family member possibly a sister or a grandmother.

In the backpack he'd brought the sixteen-ounce container of kerosene, with a tight-screwed lid. And a twelve-inch fuse, and a box of wooden matches.

In the garage behind Ms. Swale's house was a single vehicle—Ms. Swale's white Ford Taurus that had scratches and scrapes on its fenders. Most of the garage was used for storage and the car had been carefully driven into place, and parked, with but a few inches' clearance on each side.

Trash cans, gardening implements, bicycles and a single tricycle in the garage. Cardboard boxes, wicker baskets. Even an old decayed macramé planter. The windows were thick with a coating of grime and yet sunshine through one of the windows was so refracted, a transparent rainbow hovered in midair. She'd said *Your son is very gifted, Mr. Cash! Even if he has—probably—appropriated some of these images from the Internet.*

Deftly his hands worked. As if he'd performed this ritual many times before: distributed kerosene in careful dribbles about the stale-chilly space in every corner of the garage and as far beneath the Ford Taurus as he could manage, and positioned the container, with an inch or so of liquid remaining, against a cardboard box filled with Styrofoam, and attached the twelve-inch fuse to it, and, with the first swipe, lit the wooden match.

Quite an imagination! You should be proud, Mr. Cash.

On his bicycle halfway home when he'd heard the Kittatinny Falls volunteer fire alarm, wailing in the distance like a stricken and incredulous animal.

4

CHURCH OF ABIDING HOPE
TRENTON, NEW JERSEY
MAY 2012

Shall we not say, we are made in God's image?

Shall we not say—*dare to say*—we are made in the image of God's love?

This Sunday morning he'd been taken by Daddy Love to the Church of Abiding Hope in Trenton. Not often had Son been taken by Daddy Love to witness Preacher Cash among strangers.

In this congregation of mostly dark-skinned worshippers. A scattering of "whites"—single, not-young women—and among them the Preacher's son with his eerily pale putty-colored skin that was yet, to the discerning eye, a *colored skin*.

Son in a trance of wonder. Son hearing his daddy's preacher-voice so calm so consoling so subtly modulated, it was difficult for Son to believe *This man is my father!*

Reverend Silk had invited Reverend Cash to give a guest sermon in his church.

Gideon was feeling tremulous, sickish. Gideon could hear and feel his stomach rumbling in discontent with the hastily eaten cold-cereal breakfast at dawn of that day, at the faraway farm on the Saw Mill Road, Kittatinny Falls. Daddy Love had driven them in the van without stopping along the narrow twisting River Road which was Route 29 south. Daddy Love had said, You will observe silence, son, in the Church of Abiding Hope.

The Preacher lifted his hands. The Preacher's stone-colored eyes shone with an exuberant light.

Bless you my brother in Christ! Bless you my sister in Christ!

Know that we are kin in Being—inside our separate skins.

Very still Gideon sat in the front pew, to the side. It was astonishing to him—how Daddy Love had transformed himself into the Preacher who was another person, almost.

Like Daddy Love was two persons, in himself.

There was Daddy Love who cuddled and kissed and fed and comforted and there was Daddy Love whose cuddle-kissing hurt terribly and whose temper flared like kerosene bursting into flame.

There was Daddy Love who *protected*.

There was Daddy Love who *disciplined*.

Preacher Cash was a kindly man you could see. And a *kingly* man—he wore a black coat and black trousers and a brilliant white shirt but his vest was a scarlet velvet fabric. His dark beard bristled and his hair threaded with silver fell to his shoulders. He appeared taller than Daddy Love—for his backbone was straight, his shoulders very straight.

The joy of the Lord God, I bring you.

And His joy in you, His beloved children in whom He is well pleased.

In this beautiful blessed Church of Abiding Hope.

Gideon did not wish to lock eyes with the Preacher. He had been told to sit quietly and so he sat quietly with his head bowed yet observing, through his eyelashes, the Preacher moving among the congregation.

These are *starving souls* Daddy Love had told Son.

All of humankind are *starving in their souls*—except some are aware and others are not.

The seed of Jesus Christ falls upon fertile ground and upon fallow ground.

It is the task of the Preacher to bring the seed of Jesus to both the fertile and the fallow for all are brothers and sisters in Christ.

For more than thirty minutes the Preacher spoke passionately to the congregation of starving souls. No one could look away from him—all were mesmerized.

Most were women—older, dark-skinned women—festively dressed, with large flowered hats. Gideon would have estimated the average age to be about fifty. Though there were a few young children—grandchildren, with their grandmothers?

He did not have a grandfather, or a grandmother. Daddy Love said, *I am your family, Son. I am all that stands between you and the river.*

Thinking such thoughts, Gideon was feeling anxious. The sensation in his stomach had not faded.

In Trenton, there were frequent sirens. On their way to the church on State Street they'd seen both a speeding police cruiser and a speeding ambulance, each with a siren wailing.

It had been much talked-of in Kittatinny Falls—the "arson fire" in Ms. Swale's garage. Local police and sheriff's deputies were investigating the fire but had no suspects yet and now more recently there'd been two additional fires set in garages in Kittatinny Falls.

The three fires were within a radius of a mile of West Lenape Elementary School.

Daddy Love had said, reading of the fires in the local weekly paper, *You know anything about this, Son? Sounds like kids to me. Or—a kid.*

Laughing Daddy Love had said *Reminds me of something I did when I was a kid in Detroit. Burnt out some neighbors that deserved it.*

Gideon's heart had clutched at these words. But Daddy Love meant nothing by them. (Did he?)

It was hard for Son not to think that Daddy Love could read his thoughts.

Long ago, when he'd first come to live with Daddy Love as Daddy Love's "adopted" son, Daddy Love had certainly had the power to read his thoughts.

Any kind of mutinous thought, Daddy Love could discern. Son understood this!

Gideon sneered at such fear. Now he was eleven years old, no one could read *his* thoughts.

Recalling how years before in Trenton—a residential neighborhood called Grindell Park—Daddy Love had taken him to a playground in shorts and a T-shirt and he'd been allowed to play on the swings and slide and Daddy Love had drifted back to his van parked at the curb and after a time—it might have been as long as an hour, or as short as fifteen minutes—Gideon had become uneasily aware of someone observing him; a man, a stranger; standing a little distance from the playground, and then drifting about it, circling, an object in his hands that resembled a camera, possibly a video camera; and Gideon felt a wild elation swinging higher, and higher; thinking *He will take me away. He has come for me.*

There were other children in the playground, other children swinging on the swings, but their mothers were with them. Gideon was the only child who appeared to be *alone.*

After a while, Gideon stopped swinging. He was very tired and yet very excited. At the curb, the van remained. You could not see into the tinted windows even if you stood close beside it. And you would think, seeing the van parked at the curb, at Grindell Park, that there was no one inside the vehicle.

Gideon detached himself from the swing and walked in the direction of a water fountain. The man with the camera was aware of him and after a moment began to follow him.

He will take me home. To my real home.

He is a policeman, plainclothed.

From TV with Daddy Love, Gideon knew about "plainclothed" police. He knew about "undercover" police officers.

Yet, the man with the camera did not look like a police officer for he was fattish and flush-faced and seemed very nervous.

He approached Gideon in a sideways sort of walk as if he was facing another direction but his feet brought him to Gideon at the water fountain.

His voice was hoarse and drawling—H'lo little boy!

Gideon looked quickly away. Daddy Love had warned him never to speak with strangers except when Daddy Love was present and then only if Daddy Love gave him permission.

H'lo little boy—where's your mommy?

You don't have any mommy—here?

Are you alone here?

What's your name?

The man now stood beside Gideon breathing quickly and smiling down at him. He was older than Daddy Love. His black plastic glasses slid down his nose. His lips were damp.

Did your mommy leave you here and go away somewhere? That isn't a good idea, you know. Somebody had better watch over you, eh? The man took Gideon's hand. Gideon tried to pull away but the man held his hand harder.

Then it happened, Daddy Love appeared.

Daddy Love came quickly with long strides and Daddy Love's shoulder-length hair flared about his stern frowning wrathful face and the flush-faced man saw him, released Gideon's hand and turned away anxious and stumbling and Daddy Love overtook him seizing him by the shoulder and shaking him and speaking to him harshly as Gideon stared but could not hear through the roaring in his ears.

The flush-faced man tried to move away but Daddy Love walked close beside him shoving and punching at him with the flat of his hand. Daddy Love was taller than the flush-faced man who was very frightened now and apologetic.

For several minutes Daddy Love spoke with the flush-faced man but now more quietly. If the mothers in the playground noticed the men, they gave no sign.

It was late afternoon now. Most of the children had been taken home by their parents by now.

Gideon hovered at a little distance, uncertain. He was fearful of Daddy Love's wrath turning upon *him*.

At last, Daddy Love released the man, who had taken his wallet from his pocket and hurriedly removed the bills, to hand to Daddy Love who took the bills with a sneering frown, and shoved them into his pocket.

The flush-faced man hurried away limping. Daddy Love turned to Gideon and in that instant Daddy Love's face was livened by a smile.

Son! You did well. Not a word to that pervert—I saw.

My son in whom I am well pleased.

A feeling of relief and vast joy had come over Son.

Now in the Church of Abiding Hope there was a joyous feeling.

For it was a wondrous thing, that the white-skinned Preacher Cash declared himself a brother of Reverend Silk—the two ministers spoke warmly of each other as *brothers*.

And a wondrous thing, that the white-skinned Preacher Cash spoke so tenderly yet so firmly, boldly.

I say unto you my sisters and brothers in Christ—forgive your enemies. Love your enemies, as Christ has bidden us. Some will say that it is too late in our American history for my message. Some will say that the age of terrorism is not an age of love but of war, wrath, and vengeance. But I say unto you—there can be no just vengeance without abiding forgiveness, abiding hope, and abiding love.

Smiling Reverend Silk stood to the side, by the church pulpit.

Reverend Silk who was Preacher Cash's comrade and friend and who would share the collection with Preacher Cash after the service. Reverend Silk was a dark-skinned handsome man of late middle age with a look of the Reverend Martin Luther King, Jr., in his short-trimmed dark hair and the small neat mustache on his upper lip. He too was strikingly dressed in dark coat, dark trousers, white shirt and gilt-brocade vest.

A choir sang—"Coming Home to Jesus."

The choir sang in strong loud voices and the congregation joined in.

The jubilant mood in the church rose, and rose. A sensation of such goodness you wanted to cry, or to scream. You wanted to throw yourself on the floor, that the Savior would take you into his heart and up to Heaven and all the unhappiness of your life would be left behind.

There was Preacher Cash lifting his hands for a final blessing—

My sisters and brothers in the Crucifixion, the Resurrection, and Life Everlasting in Christ—AMEN.

5

NEW JERSEY TRANSIT STATION
TRENTON, NEW JERSEY
MAY 2012

Get out, Son.

Out?

Get out, Son. Do as I say.

It was a busy downtown street in Trenton—Sloan Avenue. Gideon was taken by surprise for he'd assumed that Daddy Love was driving back to Kittatinny Falls.

Politely Daddy Love had declined Reverend Silk's invitation to have a Sunday meal with him and his family. Daddy Love had said he had best be returning home, for both he and his son had tasks to be done.

Yet, only a few blocks from the Church of Abiding Hope, Daddy Love pulled the minivan up to an entrance of the New Jersey Transit Bus Station.

Gideon was confused. Gideon was frightened. But Gideon knew not to hesitate, to obey Daddy Love.

Fumbling at the door handle with numbed fingers and so Daddy Love reached across him with an impatient grunt and opened the door.

Out, Son. And inside the station.

Daddy Love was still in his Brother Cash preacher-clothing which gave to his manner an air of dignity and purpose. His hair, that fell to his shoulders in flaring, dramatic wings, smelled of hair oil, and his stiff whiskers brushed against Gideon's face.

Gideon asked what did Daddy Love want him to do in the bus station?—for Gideon did not want to think that Daddy Love was abandoning him.

Just hang out inside, Son. Sit on a bench like you're waiting for a bus.

But—will you come back for me, Daddy Love?

Gideon's voice was a piteous-Son voice.

In the Church of Abiding Hope, after the service, when the last of the congregation had left, and Brother Silk and Brother Cash were speaking together, Gideon had heard Brother Silk ask Brother Cash about him, and he'd heard the reply: My eleven-year-old, who's staying with me for now.

And he'd heard Brother Silk ask about—was the name "Deuteronomy"?

Gideon knew that "Deuteronomy" was the name of a book of the Bible. But nothing more.

Brother Cash had spoken then quietly, in a lowered voice to Brother Silk. All that Gideon could overhear was that

"Deuteronomy" had returned to live with his "godless" mother, in northern Michigan.

Now, Gideon was clutching at the door handle, fearful of leaving Daddy Love for perhaps this was what had happened to "Deuteronomy"—Daddy Love had disciplined him by forcing him to leave the minivan in a city, and driving away.

Daddy Love, you will come back—won't you?

In his Brother Cash attire, Daddy Love was not so irritable as sometimes Daddy Love was, when Son pleaded in such a way. For, in truth, Daddy Love felt tenderness in his heart, to see that the boy was so utterly broken, so unquestionably *his*.

Just go inside the station, Son. If you see a police officer, look away. If a stranger approaches you, do not speak with him.

But—will you come back for me, Daddy Love?—Gideon's voice was piteous.

He laughed, but not unkindly. He kissed Son's forehead in a blessing.

Jesus hath said, "O ye of little faith, why do you doubt?"

And Daddy Love shoved Gideon out of the minivan in front of the New Jersey Transit entrance, and drove away.

On dazed legs the boy went inside the station.

A sound as of crazed cicadas roaring in his ears.

And so many people! Mostly dark-skinned.

He thought *Daddy Love would not abandon me. Daddy Love loves me.*

There was a policeman, youngish, speaking into a little phone, making his way through the station. If his gaze moved over Gideon Cash sitting on one of the benches, beside a woman with fretting young children, it did not snag or linger.

Loud-amplified voices announced bus departures. Gideon saw lines of passengers shuffling through doors, onto buses. He thought *Daddy Love loves me best.*

Son firmly believed this. Gideon believed too but not so firmly.

Gideon knew: there had been other boys living in Daddy Love's house in Kittatinny Falls

Or anyway, there'd been predecessor-boys in Daddy Love's life because Gideon was wearing their left-behind clothes and shoes that were too big for him.

Yet Daddy Love did not like it, that Gideon *grew.*

Skinny and lanky-limbed and one of the taller boys in sixth grade.

His face was a young-boy's face. You would think no older than ten.

But his brain was no child's brain. In the night, Gideon could feel it thrumming with thoughts like something vibrating.

Son slept. Gideon lay sleepless.

Son had not the slightest doubt, Daddy Love would return to the bus station for him.

Gideon had not a doubt also. Yet, Gideon was anxious.

His eyes were fixed to a large ugly clock on a wall. His eyes were fixed to the minute hand jumping.

There was ceaseless motion in the bus station. Here and there, white-skinned passengers. And here and there, a pale-skinned boy of about his age, but never alone.

Though there were older boys, teenagers, in the bus station. And these were mostly black boys in low-slung jeans, hoodies.

Minutes passed. No one approached Gideon Cash, and no one spoke to Gideon Cash.

He was thinking of the playground in Grindell Park. And feeling now less anxious, that Daddy Love had abandoned him; for the circumstances were similar, he thought.

Waiting for a stranger to come to him. A man, attracted to a solitary lonely-looking boy in the New Jersey Transit Station.

Gideon was wearing "good" clothes—a plaid flannel shirt just slightly too big for him, dark trousers, sneakers.

These were not the mud-splattered sneakers in the closet, that Daddy Love had told him his feet would grow into.

Beside Gideon, the mother with her young children. One of the little girls was peeping at Gideon through her fingers.

He laughed, and peeped at her through his fingers.

The mother was a light-skinned Hispanic woman, with fleshy lipstick lips. She asked Gideon where he was traveling and he said Delaware Water Gap and she said she'd never heard of that. She asked if he was traveling alone and Gideon said *yes*.

She was waiting for a 1:20 P.M. bus, to Camden. Gideon said he was waiting for a 1:30 P.M. bus.

Belatedly Gideon realized that he was speaking to a stranger, which Daddy Love had forbidden. In a sudden panic he rose from his seat and walked quickly to a farther side of the bus station and sat in such a way, behind a column and a gathering of young people with backpacks, so that the surprised Hispanic woman wouldn't see him.

He was thinking what a mistake he'd made. If Daddy Love was watching him from somewhere, Daddy Love would be livid with rage.

Yet here, in his new seat, Gideon was also sitting close by a (Caucasian) woman with several fretting children. But here, he would not betray Daddy Love by getting drawn into a conversation.

Thinking of how terrified he'd been once when it had seemed to him that Daddy Love might have abandoned him. He'd been very young at the time.

Six years old and Daddy Love had taken him to a July Fourth barbecue at the house of a man named Nick—"Dominick"—on the River Road across the Delaware in Pennsylvania. Daddy Love was such a friendly person, men were always inviting him to have a drink with them, or drop by the house; most of these invitations Daddy Love declined. But these were the Paglianos —Nick Pagliano was a building contractor with an office in Raven Rock—and Daddy Love had been impressed with Nick Pagliano whom he'd met through his woman-friend at the Gift Basket in New Hope.

The barbecue, with other people, and other small children, was the first occasion of its kind for Gideon since he had come to live with Daddy Love as his *adopted son*.

The Paglianos lived in a showy-looking split-level house on a promontory above the river. Gideon had never seen such a house except in pictures or on TV and when Daddy Love turned the van up the driveway, Daddy Love had whistled through his teeth. With a grim smile he'd said to Gideon—*Novo-reech, Son. Not like us Americans who work our fingers to the bone for honest wages.*

The split-level house was made of brick, stucco, and plate glass and was set back from the twisty River Road behind a screen of evergreens. Once Daddy Love arrived, and the Paglianos welcomed him and his little boy Gideon, and they were ushered out onto a redwood deck above the river, and given barbecued hamburgers and made to feel welcome, Daddy Love had seemed to relent. *Hi! I'm Chet Cash. My son and I live just across the river.*

It was a surprise—how Chet Cash had a great time at the barbecue. Chet Cash shook hands meeting new people and Chet Cash petted the Paglianos' fattish beagle named Magic Johnson and complimented Mrs. Pagliano on her wisteria garden.

Gideon petted Magic Johnson and whispered in his ear. *Hi! I am Giden Cash, my daddy and me live across the river.*

They didn't go inside the house, for the barbecue party was outdoors on the deck and around an oblong swimming pool.

Gideon was too shy to play with other young children at the party. Daddy Love hadn't brought swim trunks for him which was just as well since Gideon shrank from swimming in the shallow end of the pool, with shrieking splashing strangers' children.

In flashes sometimes he remembered his little friends at the Montessori school. He remembered their teacher who was so very nice but he could not any longer remember her name. He remembered Mommy's hand gripping his but letting go. That was *bad Mommy*. Daddy Love had explained. *They didn't want you anymore. They sold you for adoption which is like at auction. But you are safe with Daddy Love now.*

Daddy Love didn't stay long at the barbecue for often Daddy Love was restless at such gatherings. But Daddy Love shook hands with all the guests and seemed to be making new friends as Daddy Love always did. He'd introduced himself as a *single dad*, a *part-time farmer, artist, and spiritual pilgrim in our wayward times*.

He'd also done carpentry work, he told Nick Pagliano. Maybe sometime he could do work for Nick?—cabinets were his specialty.

Daddy Love and Gideon left the party, and drove back to New Jersey by way of the Delaware Gap bridge. Daddy Love said again, with a sneering shrug, *Novo-reech, Son. Not our kind of Americans.*

And so it was a surprise to Gideon when, a few weeks later, Daddy Love took him back to the Pagliano house above the river.

Somehow, Daddy Love had learned that the Pagliano family was away. And there were flyers and advertising newspapers strewn in the blacktop driveway.

Daddy Love drove unhesitatingly up to the house, in the minivan. Daddy Love parked in the horseshoe driveway and went to the front door to ring the bell and there was no answer.

Daddy Love wore gloves and was carrying a canvas sack.

Daddy Love said, Son! We are going to play a game.

Daddy Love took Son's hand and led him to the back of the house, to the redwood deck.

And Daddy Love took Son to the door on the redwood deck, that led into the house; and at the bottom of this door was a small inset door, a dog-door that was the size of the fattish beagle and that opened inward, or outward, if the dog pushed his head against it.

At the party, Gideon hadn't noticed this little door in the regular-sized door! Though he'd petted Magic Johnson and followed him around, Magic Johnson had not used his special dog-door at the time.

Yet, Daddy Love had noticed.

There is nothing Daddy Love does not notice, Son. Always remember.

The game was: Daddy Love would help Gideon push through the dog-door on his hands and knees, and then Gideon would open the regular door by turning the knob. It was not a tight fit, for Gideon was very small and Magic Johnson was a fat-bellied dog. It was not difficult for a six-year-old to turn a doorknob and open a door and please his Daddy by doing so.

Daddy Love believed that the door locked from the inside but was not otherwise locked and this turned out to be so.

Daddy Love believed that if the burglar alarm was *on,* opening the door from the inside would not trigger the alarm; and this turned out to be so.

Still, Daddy Love was cautious entering the house, after Gideon had managed to open the door. Immediately Daddy Love went to check the burglar alarm which was operated by a square white plastic thing in the wall just outside the kitchen and from there Daddy Love went to an interior closet where he discovered sockets and plugs and these Daddy Love disconnected.

Swiftly now Daddy Love moved through the house. Whistling, laughing. What a happy mood Daddy Love was in!

Daddy Love put items in his sack—a laptop computer, silver candlestick holders, silverware—until it was almost too heavy for him to carry. So quickly Daddy Love moved through the rooms of the house he seemed to have forgotten Gideon who was left behind on his six-year-old legs, unable to keep up as Daddy Love charged up the staircase to another floor.

But Gideon had learned, Daddy Love did not like a son of his *whimpering.*

Especially, Daddy Love disciplined Son for *crying.*

Forced into the terrible *safety-box* that held him captive like a mummy and locked in for a very long time so that he couldn't help wetting his pants like a little baby which was shameful to him and disgusting to Daddy Love.

So now Son could only whisper in desperation seeing Daddy Love nowhere in sight on the second floor—*Daddy! Daddy!*

He ran along the carpeted hall. He tripped, and fell forward onto his face.

But scrambled up again at once, before Daddy Love could see and scold.

Until at last Daddy Love remembered him, and stood in the hall calling to him.

Think I'd left you? Not ever, Son.

Daddy Love will never abandon *you*.

In an upstairs bedroom that was so large, Gideon couldn't see all of it without turning his head, with an entire wall made of plate glass looking out onto the river, Daddy yanked open drawers in a bureau and kicked their contents about on the carpeted floor.

Here he discovered cash, secreted away in a woman's silk evening purse. Daddy Love counted the bills swiftly once, and then twice, like a bank teller.

Fifteen hundred dollars! Assholes.

Elsewhere there was jewelry, and a man's silk neckties, and a selection of these items Daddy Love shoved into a woman's straw tote bag, and handed it to Gideon as his responsibility for carrying back out to the minivan.

Daddy Love entered the large shining bathroom that adjoined the bedroom. Gideon had never seen a bathroom so *large*.

Daddy Love insisted that Gideon use the toilet, for it was a long drive home and he didn't intend to stop.

Daddy Love often watched Gideon at the toilet. Daddy Love observed the shy stream of yellowish liquid falling and fizzing in the toilet bowl and seemed in his unpredictable Daddy Love way strangely moved.

You are such a perfect boy, Son. If only you would never grow an inch!

Daddy Love stood beside Gideon, to urinate into the toilet himself. But Gideon shut his eyes and did not see.

Daddy Love did not flush the toilet.

Instead, Daddy Love stopped the drain in the large pale-pink-marble bathtub bordered by floor-to-ceiling mirrors on two walls. And Daddy Love turned on the faucet, so that water splashed noisily but did not run out of the tub.

Gideon sucked at his fingers, seeing this.

For this was a *bad thing* to do, he remembered being told.

Long ago he'd been told. Never never turn on a faucet so that the water will overflow the sink.

Seeing the worried look in Gideon's face Daddy Love laughed.

Christ says I bring not peace but a sword, Son.

Laughing Daddy Love led Gideon back out onto the redwood deck and out to the minivan parked in the driveway. Together Gideon and his dad loaded the rear of the van.

And all the way home, Daddy Love was in a good mood. Whistling and laughing. At the Water Gap bridge he leaned over to kiss Son on the forehead in a way that frightened Son but made him feel very relieved too for it seemed that Daddy Love did love him as he'd said since the first night.

Bless you, child. You are mine.

Son.

He woke abruptly—shamefully. He'd been dozing off.

Sometimes when he was anxious and confused and worried that Daddy Love was becoming angry with him, he became strangely sleepy and couldn't keep his eyes open or his head erect.

In the New Jersey Transit Station amid so much commotion and movement and the loud announcements of buses departing and arriving and yet—Gideon had dozed off, helplessly.

Come, Son. With me. Now.

Frowning Daddy Love loomed over Gideon. He was such a figure of dignity in his black preacher's clothes and the surprise of the crimson velvet vest, you could see strangers glancing at him and in particular women.

Gideon had the idea that Daddy Love had been in the station somewhere, observing him. As in Grindell Park when he'd been on the swings. But no one had approached him now, as the flush-faced man with the video camera had approached him, and (maybe?) this was why Daddy Love was disappointed in him.

I am not so special now. No stranger cares about me.

Before Gideon could scramble to his feet Daddy Love gripped his arm and yanked him so hard it felt as if his arm was being jerked out of its socket.

He fast-walked Gideon through the station and out the exit doors to the minivan parked a half-block away. Not caring if they almost collided with people or even that they'd caught the eye of two New Jersey Transit security cops for Daddy Love was pissed about something, and Daddy Love felt a righteous indignation rush through him like a bolt of God.

This time, unlike the time at the contractor's house in Raven Rock when he'd been a little boy of six, Daddy Love did not lean over to kiss Son on the forehead; nor did Daddy Love say in his tender cuddle-voice *Bless you child. You are mine.*

6

KITTATINNY FALLS, NEW JERSEY MAY 2012

Well, Son! Let's see what you've been doing all morning.

Daddy Love lifted the macramé tote bag in vivid red-orange to inspect the stitches.

Son held himself very still for it was never clear if Daddy Love would praise his handiwork, or pass a severe judgment.

Son could not predict.

Gideon did not trust himself to predict.

But Daddy Love was smiling. Good work, Son!

And Daddy Love ran his knuckles through Gideon's spiky hair just hard enough to hurt his scalp but it was a gentle-hurt.

Saying mysteriously, Know what, Son? Maybe it's time to expand our studio.

And later that day when Gideon was setting the table for their suppertime in front of the TV—(it was NASCAR race night)—Daddy Love said as if he'd just now thought of it: Maybe you'd like a little brother to keep you company, eh? Plenty of room in Daddy Love's house as in Daddy Love's heart.

7

KITTATINNY FALLS,
NEW JERSEY
MAY 2012

Little brother.

Keep you company.

And yet: never trust a stranger, Daddy Love cautioned.

Gideon had his (secret) friends at school. Often he counted them on his fingers: Alex, Simon, Frankie, Jennie.

Sometimes he reversed them: Jennie, Frankie, Simon, Alex.

In his sixth-grade homeroom at West Lenape Elementary these were shy quiet children like Gideon Cash. Except for Jennie they were not so smart as Gideon Cash.

At lunchtime in the noisy cafeteria or at recess outside behind the school, Gideon stayed close to his friends. If he and Jennie Farley sat together at lunch often they had little to say to each other but each felt a comfort in the other's company.

Jennie had a thin freckled face, pale red-brown hair cut short as a boy's. When she smiled, her teeth were revealed as crooked in a way to make you smile, but not in meanness.

Jennie said, Mom says to ask you if you'd like to come to my birthday party.

Gideon said, he'd like that.

But Daddy Love did not approve. Daddy Love had "looked into" Jennie Farley's family and didn't like it that her father was Dwayne Farley, a deputy with the Lenape Sheriff's Department. Nor did Daddy Love approve of Alex Trow's family for his mother was a county social worker. Such people are naturally curious—nosey.

If anyone ever questions you about your daddy, Son, tell them to talk to ME. Got that?

Yes. Gideon got that.

Alex Trow was a close friend of Gideon's too. Though the boys rarely spoke together, only just hung out together at lunchtime or recess. Alex was a particularly quiet boy who had difficulty reading—he'd told Gideon that he was "dys-lec-tic" and that his brain was wired wrong—and so Gideon helped him with reading assignments and arithmetic homework. It was amazing to Gideon, that his friend could so misspell simple words and, with numerals, write them upside down without seeming to notice.

Maybe I'm just an upside-down freak, Alex said. But he wasn't smiling.

Everybody is a freak, Gideon said. If you get to know them.

You're not, Gideon. I wish I was you.

This was so spontaneous and touching, Gideon looked away.

But you can't be me. There is only one son of Daddy Love.

Yet, maybe Alex Trow could be Son's brother? If Daddy Love was serious about a new brother.

Gideon didn't think so. The new brother would be younger than eleven, Gideon seemed to know.

Alex was a twitchy nervous boy with poor motor coordination so that sometimes, for no evident reason, he dropped his cafeteria tray, or lost his balance and fell on the stairs. Yet Alex could be coaxed—coerced—into participating in rough games at recess, on the cracked and potholed asphalt playground.

West Lenape Middle School was on the other side of the parking lot from the elementary school. Often it happened that older boys, as old as fourteen, in ninth grade, drifted over to the elementary school to torment the younger children. Elementary- and middle-school children took school buses together but Daddy Love did not want Gideon to take the school bus until he was older.

Yet, Daddy Love didn't drive Gideon to school very often now, or pick him up after school; Daddy Love wanted Gideon to bicycle to school—*to save fossil fuels.*

Older boys from the middle school were mean, mocking. Their language was threaded with obscenities in emulation of the speech of adult men and their laughter was jeering and unsettling. Gideon Cash had no idea why they disliked *him*—he'd never spoken a word to them unless provoked.

Or maybe they disliked the quieter children. Boys like Alex Trow and girls like Jennie Farley who didn't laugh at their jokes but backed away from them with frightened faces.

Once, Gideon saw his friend Alex drawn into playing dodge-ball with the older boys. He'd wanted to call to Alex, to come off the playing field—but he stood at the sidelines with other children, watching.

The game was furiously played. Boys threw the ball at one another's faces and bellies. And there seemed to be a secret agenda to the game—the younger and weaker boys, like Alex Trow, were particular targets, slow to realize until they were seriously struck by the ball.

One of the ninth-grade boys, Lyle McIntyre, who lived on the Saw Mill Road not far from Daddy Love's farm, threw the ball directly into Alex's face from a distance of about five feet. As Alex recoiled, lost his balance and fell down, and hid his face in his hands, stunned and bleeding from his nose, the other players hooted and laughed and threw the ball along the field, ignoring him.

Gideon and Jennie went to help Alex to his feet. His lower face was covered in blood, and blood was dribbling onto his shirt. He was crying, his lips trembled convulsively. Gideon and Jennie walked Alex to the school, to the nurse's office.

Asked who had hurt him, Alex sat sullen and silent.

Asked who had gotten him to play such a rough game, Alex sat sullen and silent.

It was known, if you "ratted" on anyone, you would really be singled out for punishment. So Gideon didn't tell the nurse or the school authorities who the boys were from the middle school.

Smiling thinking *Christ says I bring not peace but a sword.*

*   *   *

There was the McIntyre house which was an old converted farmhouse covered in mustard-yellow vinyl siding, where Lyle McIntyre and his younger brother Bobbie lived. Lyle was in ninth grade and Bobbie was in seventh grade. Both boys were bullies and both seemed to have taken a particular dislike to Gideon Cash.

What're you looking at, fuckface?

Who the fuck are you, fuckface?

And there was Pete Baumgarten, also in ninth grade, a burly boy who lived just inside the Kittatinny village limits, in a "ranch house" adjoining a lumberyard.

Gideon never looked openly at these boys or their friends. But he studied them, covertly.

Since the "arson fires" in the garages near Lenape Elementary School there had been no further fires or disturbances in Kittatinny Falls. Numerous persons in the neighborhood had been questioned—including several middle- and high-school boys—but no perpetrator had been arrested.

Gideon smiled thinking *Assholes!*

He had a way of speaking under his breath that was in emulation of Daddy Love and a way of flaring his nostrils, as Daddy Love did when he was righteously indignant.

Now in mild weather Daddy Love wasn't so vigilant about overseeing Gideon and allowed him to bicycle to school and home again and frequently after school Gideon bicycled along the paved streets of Kittatinny Falls, observing houses in which certain of his classmates and teachers lived and wondering what their lives were, in those houses. He had a strong impulse to ride his bicycle up a driveway, peer into a back window or boldly enter a house . . .

Hi! Am I somebody you know?

Since he'd set fires in three garages, two of them belonging to strangers, Gideon was less interested in garage fires; he was more intrigued by a spectacular act, like an explosion—a bomb set off in, for instance, the fire station, or one of the several churches in town, or one of the larger stores on Broad Street. From the Internet, without Daddy Love's knowledge—(how shocked and furious Daddy Love would be, to learn that his son surreptitiously used his computer when Daddy Love was away)—he'd downloaded recipes for simple, homemade bombs . . . Just the thought of a real explosion, bringing down an entire structure, was thrilling to him.

Hi! Just to let you know I WAS HERE.

Gideon didn't want to hurt anyone, however. (Did he?)

(At school, Ms. Swale was not so smiling and cheerful as she'd been. Jennie told Gideon that their teacher was nervous now that her house would be burnt down.)

(Jennie said she felt sorry for Ms. Swale. Gideon said *yes,* he felt sorry for Ms. Swale too.)

He'd stopped drawing and painting in study hall. Ms. Swale had asked him why and he'd said with a shrug that his daddy didn't think he should be wasting time on such crap.

"Crap! Oh, Gideon. I'm sure your father didn't say such a thing . . ."

Ms. Swale looked as if she'd been struck in the face. Gideon was overcome with a sick feeling like guilt or resentment or fury and edged away from her as politely as he could.

Often on his bicycle Gideon was drawn to the edge of Kittatinny Falls, where, on the river, there was a sprawling, boarded-up old mill in which in a long-ago time, as their teacher told them, hundreds of mill-workers had been employed manufacturing ladies' and gentlemen's footware.

Only a faded sign on the tall faded-brick building remained—PRESTON FOOTWARE "LUXURY AT LOW COST." Ghostly figures emerged out of the wall, a man in a fedora hat, a woman with blond tight-curled hair, each holding footwear in their hands, for the viewer to admire. Though the old mill had been abandoned, part of the first floor was being renovated and was to become the Kittatinny Falls Community Arts Center, if the State of New Jersey could provide funds to match private donors.

Work had begun on the renovation the previous year, but was temporarily suspended. Gideon peered through new plate-glass windows into the interior, where the old floorboards had been ripped away and new tiles had been laid in place. But the walls were unfinished, needing to be plastered.

The Kittatinny Arts Center would be in a beautiful location, everyone said. A deck running the length of the building, above the Delaware River.

A room for art exhibits. A room for folk music concerts. A room in which crafts would be taught—knitting, weaving, potting, macramé.

Chet Cash had something to do with these plans. Gideon thought so. There were volunteers to serve on the local committee, to spread the word and to help raise funds, and "Chet Cash" was one of these volunteers.

In Kittatinny Falls and elsewhere in the Delaware Valley, "Chet Cash" was known as a serious artist. Particularly, his macramé products were much admired and were said to bring in a steady if modest income to support him and his son.

From the Studio of Chet Cash.

Son was proud of helping his Daddy as he did. Macramé was not easy work and could hurt your fingers and make your eyes ache and it was hard to remain indoors so much now that the weather was nice but Son did not resent working for Daddy Love for as Daddy Love explained, he provided the macramé materials, and he provided the directions, and he sold the products to retailers.

Gideon was beginning to resent macramé! Beginning to be sick of it.

Fucking macramé! Waiting to see if Daddy Love praised or scolded.

Before, Missy had kept him company. They could work outdoors if they remained at the rear of the house. (For Daddy Love did not want strangers showing up at the house and discovering that his son was the macramé artist, not Chet Cash.) But now that Missy was gone, buried beyond the garden, there was no one for Gideon to play with when he had a few minutes' playtime; there was no one to bark excitedly, no one to wag her tail, when Gideon returned from school.

Sometimes, Daddy Love wasn't even home when Gideon returned from school. Out in the minivan—where?

He is looking for a new son. A brother for you.

8

KITTATINNY FALLS, NEW JERSEY MAY 2012

Daddy Love had said, Son. Make yourself supper and take yourself to bed and Daddy Love will be home by the time you wake up.

Son said, yes Daddy.

Gideon said, under his breath *Go to hell Daddy. You are Devil Daddy and you don't love me.*

It was exciting to plan the explosion. Prepare the bomb.

Gideon knew, lots of kids blew off their hands, parts of their faces making such bombs. The Internet was filled with scare-stories. But also stories of bombs that had detonated as planned.

You won't be prepared for the THRILL—an anonymous commentator on the Internet observed.

Your ordinary little life will be shitty from now on. That is a promise.

The bottle was a twenty-four-ounce Coke bottle he'd found at a landfill. Following Daddy Love he knew to use gloves. They watched TV together—*Cops, CSI, Forensic Files.* You had to be pretty damned stupid to touch anything with your bare hands, even a bottle that would be shattered into small pieces.

Now that Gideon was older he saw things about Daddy Love that Son had never noticed before and one of these was that Daddy Love wore gloves almost everywhere.

And Daddy Love had a drawer of gloves. Including thin rubber gloves like you'd expect a surgeon to wear.

And Daddy Love had "medical supplies"—in a lockbox in his bedroom closet. But Gideon had observed him opening it once and removing packets of pills. And Gideon observed coils of rope, handcuffs, rolls of gauze . . . He'd searched for Daddy Love's key for the box but hadn't yet found it.

He'd planned *the hit* while riding his bicycle. Daydreaming in school. These past several weeks, since the Church of Abiding Hope in Trenton, and Reverend Cash's sermon, and the vigil in the New Jersey Transit Bus Station, he'd been less interested in school and in getting good grades. He'd been less interested in being *good.*

Smirking and shrugging in class. His teacher Ms. Olson like Ms. Swale was surprised and *hurt.*

It was a weakness in people, especially in women, to be so easily *hurt.* Gideon knew now what Daddy Love meant speaking in contempt of *females.*

Daddy Love had had some sort of argument with Darlene. Maybe she'd been poking her nose into the wrong part of Daddy Love's house. Maybe she'd been needling Daddy Love about taking her out. Their raised voices were surprising to Gideon, in the stillness of his life.

Now Gideon was older, Darlene wasn't needed so much for housecleaning. Gideon prepared meals and washed dishes and mopped the kitchen floor; changed bedclothes, and did laundry in a rickety old washing machine; swept, and vacuumed; took out garbage to dump behind the old hay barn. *Good work, Son!*—Daddy Love was generous with praise.

Son beamed with pleasure. Basking in Daddy Love's praise as you'd bask in sunshine sprawled on a chilly rock.

Gideon chafed at the praise. Resented Daddy Love so obviously manipulating him.

He thinks I'm some dumb little kid. Thinks I'm a moron like everybody else.

Lately Gideon came to realize that he hadn't seen Darlene in a long time. Daddy Love never hired her to clean any longer nor did Daddy Love mention her.

He asked Daddy Love where Darlene was and Daddy Love said with a shrug, Go ask the cunt yourself, you're interested.

Cunt. This was a nasty word, uttered by the middle-school boys. The McIntyre brothers laughed at Gideon as a *skinny cunt* and Gideon had not known what this might mean until now.

Cunt—female. Something whining and disgusting about them, though you needed them for some things, unavoidably.
The cunt let go of my fingers.
The cunt blew smoke in my face.
The cunt sold me to be "adopted."

Vacuuming the house while Daddy Love was out—for Daddy Love hated the noise of a vacuum cleaner.

And there was the *safety-box* in Daddy Love's closet, laid flat upon the floor.

It was a small casket with two lids that opened: the smaller one at the top, the larger below.

It was made of smooth wood and very deftly assembled. There was even room at the foot of the box for the occupant's small feet.

Daddy Love had made it himself, he'd said. For Daddy Love was a skilled carpenter.

Inside, there was cushioning, but it had become badly stained.

The *safety-box* was too small for Gideon of course. It had never been used on *him*.

He could remember: a little boy forced into the wooden box, and locked in it. He could remember: the stupid little boy crying, crying and crying which only made things worse inside the box, when the top was shut and locked, and you couldn't breathe.

He'd pissed himself. And worse.

That was the punishment: fouling yourself.

And being trapped inside the box for how long, you would never know.

What had happened to that stupid pathetic little boy, Gideon wondered.

He had been kept at a distance from the snot-nosed boy. *He* had always been treated kindly by Daddy Love.

The little boy had screamed, when the gag was removed.

When Daddy Love cuddled hard, in Daddy Love's bed.

Oh it hurt so *bad*. Between the little boy's tender buttocks, *so bad.*

And Daddy Love screamed too, a quick harsh cry like death. And a shudder ran through Daddy Love's body that was naked, and sweaty, and smelled of the little boy's blood dribbling out of his insides.

He hadn't seen. *He* hadn't been anywhere near but in another part of the house.

Now, Gideon shut the closet door. The *safety-box* had nothing to do with him.

Gideon continued vacuuming. There was a pleasure in vacuuming. Inside the noise of the vacuum, there was laughter. Gideon was laughing. Gideon's teeth were chattering, and laughing. Gideon was upset, and shivering. Gideon's bladder ached with a sudden need to pee. Almost it was painful, like a knife-stab, this need to pee. In his haste to get to the bathroom Gideon tangled his feet in the God-damned vacuum cleaner hose and nearly fell down.

Carefully he'd prepared the bomb! In a swoon of expectation bicycling into town thinking it was risky as hell, the bottle-bomb in his backpack, but he liked that feeling of risk.

Daddy Love craved *risk*. It was how Daddy Love felt *most alive* he'd said.

It was a warm sunny May afternoon. There had been no school today—some state teachers' meeting. Whether Gideon went to school or not didn't seem to matter any longer for Daddy Love had ceased coming to PTA events and never inquired after his grades no matter how high they were, or how low; and if Gideon skipped school Daddy Love had taught him to write his own excuse for his teacher and even to sign *Chester Cash*.

Gideon's homeroom teacher said, You are missing school frequently, Gideon. Is your father taking you to a doctor?

Gideon mumbled *yea, sure.*

There's nothing wrong at home, is there, Gideon?

Nah.

Maybe he should bomb the school? West Lenape Elementary? Or—the middle school? Where the McIntyre boys went.

But his plan was the mill. PRESTON FOOTWARE on the river.

Too many people might see him prowling about the schools which were in a neighborhood of small residential homes.

In Kittatinny Falls Gideon avoided the main streets and bicycled to the edge of town, to the old PRESTON FOOTWEAR mill on the river.

The ghost-lady and ghost-gentleman! Especially the female with her cap of curly blond hair and vacuous eyes holding aloft a stupid shoe offended him.

But here was a surprise: teenaged boys were at the river, clambering over large boulders. They'd left their bicycles in the weedy graveled parking lot of the mill.

Gideon wasn't sure how to proceed. He didn't recognize the boys, and they hadn't seen him yet. If he was careful, and kept to the farther side of the mill, no one would see him.

He thought *They will be killed, maybe.*

He felt a thrill of anticipation. The brick mill would explode and bricks would rain down upon the boys below, at the river's shore. They would be trapped and could not escape, the explosion would take place within seconds.

He was walking his bicycle now, in the graveled parking lot. It occurred to him that riding in so bumpy a terrain might activate the explosives in the bottle.

He had no choice but to continue to the farther side of the mill, which had been boarded up. The renovated part of the mill was at the front. This was a disappointment: he wanted to blow up the renovated part of the mill, more than the old, moldering part. But then, if the bomb was powerful enough, it would bring down the entire building.

He thought so. Maybe.

Really, he had no idea. Maybe the bomb wouldn't even go off!

But here was an advantage: the rear of the mill was accessible, if you squeezed through a fissure in a wall. The front of the mill was locked tight so he'd have had to place the bomb outside rather than inside as he could do at the rear, crawling on hands and knees with a quickened heartbeat and hearing, in the near distance, the boys at the river's shore shouting and laughing.

His hands were trembling, removing the bottle from his backpack.

It weighed very little. It could not be much of a bomb, weighing so little.

Drano—(which stank, and made his eyes water)—and strips of tin foil—inserted in the bottle. The idea was, a "chemical reaction" would occur if the heat inside the bottle increased sufficiently, which it would do if Gideon placed it in the sun.

Stealthily Gideon made his way through the ruins of the old mill, to a window opening above the river. Here, there were only shards of glass remaining. On all sides, cobwebs, dust and grime. The boys were below, noisy and obnoxious. Gideon saw that they had fishing poles. They were not boys he knew, probably high-school boys. In bright sunshine Gideon positioned the bottle on the windowsill.

He'd forgotten to wear gloves! He had meant to wear gloves but had forgotten but maybe it wouldn't matter for the bottle would shatter into bits. No one would suspect *him*.

In the local papers, it was stated that the "suspect" of the arson fires was believed to be an adult male, Caucasian, who'd been employed in Kittatinny Falls but had lost his job and moved away. An eyewitness claimed to have seen him in the vicinity of the third of the fires, on Pitcairn Street; he was driving a green pickup truck. However, this "suspect" had not yet been apprehended by the police.

Gideon's teeth were still chattering. He was cold, and shivering.

He thought *It will go off now. My hands, my face.*

He thought *Daddy Love will not love me again ever.*

The bottle was upright, but maybe the bottle would better be positioned on its side, Gideon thought, for more sunshine could concentrate upon it that way.

He turned the bottle onto its side. But now, the danger was that the bottle might roll off the windowsill . . .

He found a brick-fragment, to secure the bottle on its side. He was breathing quickly, shallowly. It was mesmerizing, to see how sunshine seemed to focus, like a laser ray, onto the bottle-bomb.

He wondered how long it would require, before the temperature inside the bottle rose high enough to detonate the explosive.

Wished he'd had someone to plan this with! He needed a friend, like Daddy Love.

Son, you are always in my thoughts. As I am in yours.

Backing away from the bottle-bomb on the windowsill. It looked so *small.*

He was disappointed, the damned bomb was *so small.*

Stumbled against some machinery, tripped and nearly fell.

But quickly righted himself, for he was an agile eleven-year-old. Not clumsy like Son.

The interior of the old mill was a ruin. There'd been a flood of the Delaware River not long ago, and the mill had been devastated. This was before the renovation had begun. Gideon wondered if, if he died in this place, anyone would ever find him.

Daddy Love would find another son. Daddy Love would not miss him for long.

He squatted on his heels, waiting. About twenty feet away the bottle-bomb on the windowsill glinted, shimmered and shone with sunshine.

How hot was it in the mill? Maybe in the high eighties? And in the sun—in the nineties?

A "chemical reaction" would take place. Gideon wondered what this meant, exactly.

Outside, on the riverbank, the boys' voices lifted.

Bicycling out to the Saw Mill Road. For he'd given up waiting.

It was late afternoon now. Soon, dusk.

He was anxious, edgy, disappointed, itchy inside his clothes, and *pissed.*

In the vicinity of the God-damned mill he'd waited—how long?—maybe an hour. He'd watched the boys fishing. He'd wished he was one of them. It seemed to him so easy, he might have been born one of *them.*

Then bicycled on nearby streets waiting for the explosion.

God-damn bomb! Fucking Internet, you couldn't trust.

At last he'd given up. For he didn't want to attract attention, a boy riding a bicycle aimlessly in a neighborhood in which he didn't live.

All the way home waiting to hear an explosion in the distance and a sound of sirens as he'd been so thrilled to hear when he'd set the garage fires.

But there was nothing.

God-damn bomb was a *dud*.

And when he returned home, there was nothing: no Missy to rush at him, tail thumping and eyes alight with love, and no Daddy Love for Daddy Love had driven away in the minivan saying *Make yourself supper, Son, Daddy Love will be home by the time you wake up.*

He checked Daddy Love's closet: the *safety-box* was gone.

9

KITTATINNY FALLS, NEW JERSEY
MAY 2012

Daddy Love asked, how'd Son like to go digging for treasure?

This was a Daddy Love game, Son supposed and so brightly Son replied.

Yes Daddy.

Gideon wasn't so sure. Gideon saw that Daddy Love was looking hot-skinned, edgy. His face was sweaty and his eyes were showing white above the dark rim of his irises. And his hands were shaky, with nervousness or excitement.

The night before Daddy Love had returned home late in the minivan after Gideon was in bed and he had not entered Gideon's room as he sometimes did to kiss him good night and play a Game of Tickle—it was a long time now since Daddy Love had kissed Gideon good night and played a Game of Tickle with him. And Gideon had lain in bed hearing sounds in Daddy Love's room which he could not interpret.

Was Daddy Love talking to himself? Did Daddy Love have the TV turned on, high?

Gideon thought *He has brought a little boy home with him. In the* safety-box.

Son had no such thoughts. For Son was all brightness and shining eyes and a yearning to be loved by Daddy Love even if the love came hurtful and hard and caused his insides to bleed out onto the bedclothes.

Take up the shovel, Son.

They went out. Daddy Love led the way. Through the ruins of the garden which Daddy Love seemed to have forgotten this spring, hadn't instructed Gideon in what to plant, or provided him with plants or seeds. Through the ruins of the garden and through the ruins of the old apple orchard in which on this warm May morning bees were buzzing and small birds were calling to one another.

Daddy Love seemed preoccupied. Daddy Love was frowning and chewing at his lower lip.

In the night, Gideon had heard some sounds. Gideon had not slept much in the night.

Stupid little boy would be gagged. Screaming inside the gag and pissing his pants like a baby.

Gideon had known better than to make noise, himself. Knew better than to call attention to himself. Not long ago, now that he no longer fit into the *safety-box*, he'd had to be chained by the neck as Missy had been chained, as a discipline.

It hadn't been clear why Daddy Love had felt the need to discipline him. This has been shortly after the trip to Trenton when many things seemed to have changed.

Daddy Love had said, There is some mutiny in your heart, Son. This is a fair warning of what to expect if it comes out. Daddy Love had chained him with Missy's chain. Chained to the stairway railing, that would not budge if Gideon yanked at it hard enough to break his neck.

Another time he'd fucked up one of the macraméd purses attaching the clasp upside down and Daddy Love hadn't noticed until his woman-friend at the Gift Basket pointed it out.

On the hike into the countryside, into an area of scrubby hills and shallow creek beds, Daddy Love led the way as Gideon struggled behind dragging the shovel.

Daddy Love was wearing a backpack. Gideon wondered what was inside the backpack.

That morning, he hadn't heard anything inside Daddy Love's bedroom. But of course, the stupid little boy would be *gagged*.

Daddy Love did not like crying, screaming, shrieking.

Except sometimes, Daddy Love did like crying, screaming, shrieking.

On the hike, Gideon began to sweat. Rivulets of itchy sweat ran down his sides, beneath his T-shirt. He was wearing shorts, and sneakers with no socks.

It was a wild place to which Daddy Love was taking him. He seemed to know, other sons had been brought to this place.

Deuteronomy—that had been the name of a predecessor. He knew this without recalling how he knew.

Son. We can stop here.

They had hiked about a mile. They'd come to a stop in a sandy-pebbly place. On the banks of an old creek bed now lush with cattails were outcroppings of shale like broken crockery. Oddly shaped boulders were strewn about, with shallow indentations that suggested ghost-faces in the stone.

Gideon thought *This is where they are buried. He has brought a knife to kill me.*

Instead, Daddy Love instructed Gideon to begin digging.

You dig for a while, Son. Then, I can take over.

Dig your own grave, Son.

Son stabbed at the earth with the shovel. Pushed down on the shovel with his foot. He was very hot, panting. He saw in the corner of his eye Daddy Love observing him, stroking his whiskers. On his head Daddy Love wore a baseball cap pulled low.

Gideon's heart was pounding faster and faster. Almost, he could not catch his breath.

Daddy Love had slipped off his backpack. A bottle of Evian water he offered to Gideon and gratefully Gideon took it. He could not see any flash of a knife blade inside the backpack.

He would dig a little longer. A little deeper into the earth. Was the treasure here? Daddy Love had seemed to have forgotten the treasure.

Gideon turned blindly, wielding the shovel. *Whack!* came the shovel down onto Daddy Love's head, and Daddy Love staggered, and fell to his knees, and the shovel was knocked out of Gideon's hands.

Gideon began to run.

Daddy Love had a knife but not the rifle. Daddy Love was too dazed to pursue him or even to shout after him.

Daddy Love's forehead was bleeding. A tributary of blood down his face, the last memory Gideon would have of Daddy Love.

On terrified feet he ran, ran.

10

YPSILANTI, MICHIGAN
MAY 2012

Mommy, I don't like her to look at me.

Josh! That's very rude.

Don't *like her*.

The child wriggled out of his mother's arms and ran away, toward his little friends in the playground.

Dinah, I'm so sorry. I can't understand . . .

It's all right, Katie. Really. *I* understand.

Dinah laughed to show that she wasn't hurt. And really, after six years, she wasn't.

In his place I'd run, too. Scarred vampire-woman without a child of her own, enough to terrify any kid.

She was a volunteer at the National Registry of Missing Children, Ypsilanti branch. The storefront organization was in Kendall Square and close by was Curries 'n' Spice where she bought lunch, vegetarian-tofu salads she ate with a white plastic fork. It was a phenomenon to her, *appetite.*

Six years after Robbie, most food still tasted like mulched cardboard. Yet the brain is so conditioned, when she saw food she'd once liked, and had once eaten with pleasure, her brain signaled her *Eat!* though she knew that the food was just the usual mulched cardboard.

Was this a fact of human mental life? Had she penetrated some small shabby truth of the human psyche?

Our memories goad us to repeat the past, when we'd been happy. Even as we know that the past is past, and we will not be happy.

The very playground to which she'd taken Robbie.

Of course, six years later none of the young mothers in the park remembered Robbie Whitcomb.

She knew most of the young mothers. They knew *her.*

A new generation of small children had come into being, since Robbie. A fact of such simplicity seemed to confuse and baffle her who had wished for time to halt when her child had been taken from her.

For, at first, it had been a matter of mere *days.* And then, *weeks.*

She had not given up hope—of course. The desperate do not give up hope, it is a proof of their desperation.

In the playground she sat with Rhoda, Tracey, Evan. These were stylish young mothers who had, among them, two Ph.D.'s and a post-doc in microeconomics. Their children were all younger than five.

Eating her tofu lunch and sipping from her bottle of Evian water.

Dinah Whitcomb is so friendly, it's hard to avoid her.

You feel guilty as hell avoiding that poor woman.

Dinah's generation of young mothers in this park had long moved on. Their children were in middle school now, or older. Though from time to time Dinah saw, or thought she saw, a young mother from that time, who seemed, glancing at Dinah, and quickly away, to recognize her.

Her son was never found? How many years has it been?

The look in her eyes. It's hard to bear.

In fact, Dinah Whitcomb was a source of much merriment. She laughed a good deal, and she inspired laughter in others. She did not ever speak of her own situation, nor did she allude to it. Like one who is tethered to an enormous boulder, which she must drag with her when she moves, she felt no obvious need to speak of her disability but rather more an instinct to make light of it.

Her worst days, she still used a cane. But this was rare.

She walked *swaying*. But God damn, she *walked*.

In the park, at lunchtime, talking and laughing with the young mothers, as if she were not a woman now of thirty-four and no longer young and no longer a mother.

As she talked and laughed with Rhoda, Tracey, and Evan she watched their children playing together at the sandbox. In a paralysis of yearning and wonderment she watched. When she'd had Robbie, in this park, she'd been so caught up in the minutiae of young-motherhood, like a swimmer in a turbulent sea, she hadn't had much awareness of herself, as she had now; for now, nothing seemed so astonishing to her as the fact that, six years before, she'd been one of these young mothers *and she had not grasped the miracle.*

Now, it took her breath away.

The children were so beautiful! So funny, needy, exasperating, endearing . . .

She could not ever tell these young mothers what frightened her: that she'd begun to forget what Robbie looked like. That she needed to page through the albums, to hold the snapshots to the light, to recall.

This forgetfulness had begun soon after the neurological damage. Yet Dinah did not think it was neurological but a failing of spiritual strength.

That was her terrible secret: her unworthiness.

Eleven years old! She felt faint and sick, she could not imagine her son now.

Poor Dinah! They should've had another baby.

Either that or kill yourself. I mean—what could you do?

The children's cries over-excited her. The children digging in the sandbox, playing at the teeter-totter, as Robbie had done. There was always a boy very like Robbie . . . That morning she'd driven out of her way for the first time in more than a year to pass, slowly, the Montessori school where her son had been enrolled six years before.

It was never such a wild stretch of the imagination that Robbie would be waiting for her at the rear, with his little friends . . .

Talking and laughing and trying not to recall. One of her rueful little anecdotes involving *my husband*.

She meant to be entertaining. The women knew Whit Whitcomb who was a quasi-public figure in Ypsilanti–Ann Arbor, host of local fund-raisers, co-chair of the annual spring Walk-A-Thon for Memorial Children's Hospital and more recently the Walk/ Bark for Autism—a ten-mile hike through the University of Michigan arboretum in which dog owners and their dogs participated, with much publicity and success.

He hadn't wanted another child. He hadn't wanted to try.

In secret, she'd tried. But she had not succeeded.

It was a spiritual failing, she believed. Not physical, or not physical merely.

She was losing the train of her thought. She'd been entertaining her friends with a story about an experiment in one of her social psychology laboratories, but she was losing the point of the anecdote, and sensing their discomfort. *That poor woman! She can't stop talking.*

It was the proximity of the children here in the playground. Their high sharp cries were distracting to her. Already six years before these *live children* had begun to replace Robbie in the world.

She stammered and fell silent. The others were silent, abashed.

She snatched at the Evian water, drank and dribbled water down her chin.

Her mother had said of her in sharp disappointment *Dinah! You've let yourself go.*

In Geraldine McCracken's vocabulary that was the worst you could do—*let yourself go.*

It was very hard to confront herself in a mirror. The most torturous were three-way mirrors at rehab.

Papery-thin scar tissue in layers. The thin-lashed eyes like eyes peering through a mask. Her face was the most subtle of Hallowe'en horror-masks since it mimicked actual skin.

The *uncanny valley* in which the degree of the unbearable increases as the nonhuman approaches the look of the human. Dinah had learned of the *uncanny valley* in her graduate psychology course and had wanted to say to the professor wittily, Hey I live there!

In a paroxysm of itching she'd scratched, scratched, scratched her face while sleeping and woke confused and bleeding and there was Whit staring at her in horror.

Dinah. My God.

There was the impulse to scratch with her fingernails now. But Dinah would not.

Not in public: no scratching her face, no touching. No feeling-sorry-for-herself.

It was time to leave Admiral Park. She must not stay long.

She'd hoped for a quick little farewell to one of the children—a hug, a kiss—but this wasn't going to happen, it seemed. For the children were at the sandbox and it would seem very odd for her to approach them.

Her face frightened them. The just-perceptible misalignment of her jaw, and the focus in her right eye.

In the street, she often saw people staring at her. And at the university where she'd re-enrolled in a graduate program in social psychology.

Either they knew who she was, or suspected.

Or they had no idea who she was but were startled by her appearance.

When she rose to leave, one of the young mothers leapt up to help her, for her right knee buckled in pain.

Her awkward body quivering in pain, she would not acknowledge.

Her face draining of blood she laughed in farewell. Bravely she walked away.

Knowing that they were looking after her, pitying her. Knowing they would be speaking of her.

Poor Dinah! She just talks, talks . . .

Is she on medication, do you think?

Oh God. What hell for her. And her husband . . .

Do you think she talks like that all the time? At home?

It was true, Dinah talked too much. Dinah talked without listening to her own scratchy voice. Dinah prized those moments when a listener smiled and laughed. When she'd *amused*.

It was an addiction of hers, Whit said.

She'd forced herself to give up her prescription of OxyContin, Vicodin. She limited herself to Tylenol for pain and for sleepless nights. She didn't allow herself to drink as much as a glass of wine—if she began, she might not be able to stop.

Haunting parks, playgrounds. Even the Libertyville Mall. And driving past the Montessori school. These were the addictions. Her volunteer work was more plausibly integrated into her adult life. It was addictive too, but it was of genuine use to others. Whit didn't criticize Dinah's volunteer work. But his own volunteer work did not overlap with hers any longer.

Crossing a street from Admiral Park she nearly lost her balance. But for her pride, she'd have brought her cane.

Ma'am? You needin some help?

Thank you, no. I'm—fine.

Dubiously the girl watched her. Jamaican, young, in the white uniform of a medical worker.

Whit had said, take the damn cane with you, at least! It's just your pride, plenty of people use canes.

Her mother hated seeing Dinah with the cane. Still more, with the walker. Oh Dinah look at you! My *daughter.*

When she rose to her feet after sitting for a while, there was often a roaring in her head. It would require a few minutes for Dinah to get her bearings, it was *not serious.*

She'd had MRIs. No further neurological damage had been discovered in the injured part of her brain.

In recent months she'd had another brain scan, an echocardiogram, an angiogram, a colonoscopy, and much bloodwork.

She continued with physical therapy, intermittently. She'd ceased seeing a psychotherapist, as Whit had. There was no point, for there was nothing wrong with either of them that the return of their lost son would not remedy.

The fact is, she'd let Robbie go. She'd had his hand firmly in hers and then . . .

A therapist will work with you on issues of *guilt*. But a therapist cannot work with you on the primary issue, the reversal of the situation that has caused *guilt*.

The children in the playground had over-excited her, that was it. For always there was one who might have been Robbie seen from the back, or the side . . .

Always there was one whose voice, heard at a little distance, uplifted, elated, excited, was Robbie's voice . . .

Mommy? Mom-my!

And somehow, the child-voice was her own. So wistful!

Mom-my . . .

Her mother e-mailed links to Dinah, Web sites and home pages involving other missing children. For there were so many.

And when Geraldine visited, and Whit wasn't near, Geraldine was likely to unfold for Dinah a newspaper article from the *Detroit News* about a child-abduction in, for instance, New Mexico, or Florida, or North Dakota—*7-Year-Old Taken from Backyard, No Witnesses.*

And, *10-Year-Old Abducted by Car-Jacker, Mother in Hospital.*

Please don't show me these things, Mother—so Dinah begged.

In these six years, Geraldine too had aged. But you would have to see her near-flawless face in a harsh light, and to consider the tight, taut skin around her eyes, to register this fact.

It was one of the prevailing subjects of which the young mothers in the park spoke: their mothers, and their mothers-in-law.

Inescapably, a world of women. Dinah recalled a play of the English Renaissance—*Women Beware Women*.

Or was the title *Women Betray Women*.

Possibly it was rude, yes of course it was rude, but everyone did it, the young mothers, and not-so-young Dinah Whitcomb: checking for cell phone messages, e-mail.

Though Dinah Whitcomb checked more compulsively than the others.

Dozens of times a day. Always with hope.

For one day the news would come. One day, the vigil would end. She had no doubt. Not for a moment.

Unlike Whit who said with a savage laugh, he doubted the very ground upon which he walked.

Back at the Missing Children center she managed to collapse at her desk. It was a plain bare battered Salvation Army desk with a landline—the "hotline" that rarely rang. How weak she felt, like water rushing out of a drain. Voices came to her at a distance. Why do we care for other people, why do we love them, grieve for them, yearn for them, require them?—when we will die alone, far from them.

So weak! She could rest her heavy head on her crossed arms, hide her ruined face against the desktop and sleep and never wake.

Dinah? Dinah? *Dinah?*

Never wake.

* * *

Leila said, Oh! let me see it.

He showed her. One of the colored chalk portraits.

What a beautiful child . . . His name was—Robbie?

He smiled. He smiled in order not to say something very cutting to her.

His name *is* Robbie.

Oh yes I mean—*is*.

Six years before, Whit had taken up sketching. He'd always had a predilection for drawing, a facile talent for cartooning and caricaturing, but when Robbie was taken from them, and photographs of Robbie were publicly posted, Whit began sketching his son with colored chalks based upon memory as well as photographs. It had been Whit's intention to update Robbie's portrait with the passage of time but he hadn't been so successful at this and eventually gave up.

The Michigan State Police and the FBI provided "updated" photo-images of Robbie from time to time but these uncanny images were discomforting to Whit and Dinah. Especially to Dinah who reacted emotionally.

There was something robot-like about the updated images of his son. As if an alien being had insinuated itself inside five-year-old Robbie Whitcomb and was forcing his child-body into a new shape, and his child-face into a new face, a stranger to his parents.

Robbie's room was more or less untouched. Whit knew that Dinah entered the room at least once each day but he had no idea what she did in the room or how long she remained in it.

Whit very rarely stepped inside, though the door was always kept open.

The most obvious change was, they'd removed the disturbing posters they had not liked. In their place, they'd substituted Whit's colored-chalk portraits of Robbie.

Whit would have liked to move out of the house—it was too small, ordinary, confining. He'd had too many sleepless nights here and too much anguish. The early memories of his feckless happy fatherhood had been abraded by more recent memories of disgust, fury.

He'd have liked to move ten miles west to Ann Arbor where he had many friends and far more admiring listeners to his radio program than he had in Ypsilanti.

But Dinah refused. To move away from this house, from Robbie's room, was to abandon Robbie.

Whit didn't argue with Dinah. Whit tried to respect Dinah's beliefs—her superstitions.

His smart sardonic wife. Now attending services at the Community of Christ Church, Ypsilanti.

(To her credit, Dinah was embarrassed about this. Dinah didn't want Geraldine, a long-lapsed Catholic, to know.)

(It was just for the *atmosphere*, Dinah had told Whit. Singing, holding hands, rejoicing in being alive, *not thinking*.)

Carmella had said, You can't ever leave her, Whit. Because you'd be leaving *him*.

Whit didn't dispute this. In his vanity he'd wanted to think that a woman like Carmella Fontaine who was artistic director at an experimental Ann Arbor dance-theater would remain with him, in love with him, indefinitely.

After Carmella there'd been others. He was so lonely, so despairing!

His sexual being, the very essence of his soul, had been obliterated, at the time of his son's abduction. His sense of himself as an individual with some degree of control over his life had vanished utterly. His fatherhood, his manhood, his dignity. Another man, a predator, had taken his *son*.

It might have been the most ancient and primitive of insults, Whit thought. More even than the abduction of a wife.

For wasn't the Biblical story of Abraham and Isaac the most terrifying of all Bible stories, in making of a loving father an accomplice to a wrathful God?

And there were the injuries to Dinah.

Rarely had Whit tried to make love with his wife for he feared hurting her. And he felt—well, he didn't feel anything like his old desire for her, that had been obliterated forever, however brave and sexily brash poor Dinah might try to present herself.

We need another baby, Whit. Please.

Dinah, you're not well.

I am well. Women far more disabled than I am have gotten pregnant and given birth.

You're not strong enough. We've been through this.

We've discussed it, but—we haven't been *through this.* When Robbie comes home, whenever that is, he would expect to see a younger sister or brother—it's only natural. He would expect a *family.*

This was so utterly insane, Whit couldn't trust himself to reply.

Gotten pregnant was an expression that particularly revolted him. How did a woman *get pregnant,* was it something one did for oneself? With a syringe, an eyedropper?

Another new craziness of Dinah's was vegetarianism.

Her revulsion for meat, for the very sight of meat, and the idea of meat—*enslavement and slaughter of innocent animals.* On several occasions at friends' houses Dinah had become white-faced and nauseated by the smell of grilling meat, had had to excuse herself and rush away staggering to a toilet.

Great company they were, the Whitcombs!

All the more intolerable since Whit Whitcomb so loved bar-becued ribs, sushi, roast pig, beef tartar, rack of lamb and the better cuts of steak.

The fact was, he'd come to hate Dinah.

The fact was, he loved Dinah. Of course he loved Dinah. It was a vow he'd taken, he would always love Dinah McCracken and he would always protect her from harm.

Dinah and Robbie. His love for his wife and his son had come so powerfully, he'd felt faint as one inhaling odorless but highly potent fumes. He had not ever loved anyone in his life as he'd loved them—he hadn't been adult enough for such love, until the birth of his son.

Yet, he was drifting inexorably from Dinah like one in a boat without oars, drifting from another oarless boat. For a while the stream had borne the two boats in the same direction but now the current was changing, the two were separating.

After six years he was burnt-out. His way of grieving had been to actively look for the abductor, to keep calling the Ypsilanti police and the Michigan State Police and the FBI, to print up new flyers, to go on TV and make his appeal. And again, and again—this had been Whit Whitcomb's way for it was his way too of staying sane.

His way was not to lie on the child's bed curled into a fetal position sleeping through much of the daylight. Not to attend evangelical Christian church services and sing hymns holding hands with strangers and crying together.

A baby. Paraplegic women can have babies. Let me show you on the Internet.

Whit, please! When Robbie comes back to us he would expect a more normal kind of family.

To the casual glance, Dinah didn't seem incapacitated. So long as she was seated, and talking—*talking* was what Dinah did, with much animation—not on her feet, trying to walk with her old ease and grace.

To the casual glance, Dinah didn't seem disfigured. She appeared to be a few years older than her age, which was thirty-four; she'd gained weight steadily, since a low of one hundred pounds, and now weighed, Whit guessed, as much as one hundred thirty-five pounds. Her shoulders and upper arms were muscular from rehab and weight lifting and those many months when she'd eased the pain-causing pressure on her lower body by walking with a cane, or a walker, or propelling herself about—("propelled" was Whit's admiring word)—using counters, backs of chairs, tabletops and railings, like one of those disabled Olympic athletes who perform competitively, and aggressively. Her legs were relatively weak, and thin; her right knee was particularly susceptible to pain. She had migraine headaches that left her blinded, exhausted. She had difficulty typing at a computer and using a pen. She'd built up her injured body around her disabilities as a tree grows stunted yet triumphant around an impediment.

Whit was proud of Dinah: she'd had months of excruciating physical therapy and had not ever complained. She was now far better coordinated than she'd been five years ago when the doctors' prognosis had been so poor. What upset Whit was, she insisted upon thinking of herself as strong when in fact she wasn't strong: she collapsed easily, and had been rushed to the ER more than once, hyperventilating, or stricken with a violent tachycardia, or afflicted with a paralyzing gastrointestinal pain. She insisted upon thinking of herself as *near-normal.*

It was Dinah's God-damned pride, she rarely used her cane. Though Whit had bought her a fancy Victorian cane beautifully carved out of ivory.

(She'd said, How the hell can I walk with an *ivory cane?* An elephant was slaughtered for this ivory, Whit!)

And her pride, she insisted upon walking from the parked car, rather than having Whit drop her off as he'd gratefully have done. And inevitably she faltered, and had to rest clutching at Whit's arm—No, no! I'm fine. I just get a little—winded, sometimes . . .

Often, Dinah hid her face from Whit. It made her anxious when he looked frankly at her and it made her anxious when he seemed to be averting his eyes from her.

She didn't apologize for her face, at least. Whit would have been furious with her if she'd tried.

In fact her face didn't repel him. Beneath the translucent scarry tissue was Dinah's true face. And the beautiful dark-brown eyes thin-lashed and unchanged.

Geraldine said slyly to him, when Dinah was out of the range of her lowered voice, D'you think we don't know? We know.

He'd wanted to shove the woman from him. Always her manner with Whit Whitcomb had been subtly mocking, flirtatious. She'd never tried to address Whit as her daughter's husband and the father of her daughter's child, only as "Whit" Whitcomb who was some sort of disc-jockey charlatan with a weakness for pot and for casual sex. This character could pull the wool over others' eyes, but not hers.

Hotly she said, *She* knows but she won't say a thing. Because that's Dinah's nature—weak, trusting. At least you could be more circumspect.

And when Whit didn't dignify this bullshit by replying, she said meanly, That means—*evasive*. At least you could be more—

I know what *circumspect* means, Geraldine. Thanks!

He would leave Dinah, maybe. For this would be a way of leaving the bitch of a mother-in-law, too.

He would leave Dinah but not until her physical condition was stronger. And not until Robbie returned.

239

And if Robbie did return, if the miracle happened, certainly Whit Whitcomb wasn't going to leave his wife and son.

In this way they waited.

For six years, they'd waited.

The mother waited with more evident faith that the child would be returned to them, the husband with conspicuously less.

Yet, they had only to glance at each other, at times, to be immediately linked, bonded.

The sight of a child on the street, a stray remark made by a stranger, the appearance of someone who reminded them of, for instance, one of the Ypsilanti detectives to whom the missing-child case had been assigned, years ago—these were triggers.

Sometimes, Dinah burst into tears for no evident reason. Whit knew the reason.

She told him her dreams. He rarely told her his.

Yet it was uncanny, sometimes their dreams overlapped.

In her dreams, Robbie was frequently a presence. But where Robbie's face was, were blurs like eraser smudges. The terror came over her—*I am forgetting his face.*

In the dreams Robbie was being returned to them. Yet, there were invariably complications. Dreams that went on and on *and on* like endless journeys on badly rutted roads in bad weather.

How many times Dinah had felt the child's fingers wrenched from hers! How many times she'd been thrown to the ground and yet fantastically caught up beneath the abductor's minivan in a way to drag her along the pavement like a limp lifeless rag doll . . . Recounting these dreams to Whit she described her sleep interrupted by the droning voices of strangers, recorded phone-voices, computer-voices; there were endless documents and forms for the bereft parents to fill out; a jarring squawk of radio-voices; bright fluorescent lights searing her eyes. Until suddenly it would be revealed to her that Robbie wasn't there, and had never been there.

And Whit would think *But that was my dream!*

Since she'd become a hotline volunteer Dinah had particularly exhausting nightmares in which she was on the phone trying to hear a faint, fading voice—(Robbie's voice?)—pleading and screaming for the party not to hang up.

Don't abandon me! Don't abandon *me.*

Yet Whit stayed away from the house as long as he could. *He could not help it, this was his addiction.*

He'd waked from the nightmare to find himself a (minor, local) celebrity. Whenever any child-abduction case erupted as breaking news, "Whit" Whitcomb was likely to be quoted in print or interviewed on TV. His was a whirligig-life in terror of solitude and silence: work, busyness, sex, drinks with friends, occasional pot, even seeing late-afternoon movies at the mall, alone. "Action" movies of brainless and relentless violence which Dinah could not have tolerated.

Dinah was lonely but never criticized him. She must have taken a vow, she would never criticize her companion in bereavement.

Her less frantic life mimicked his, to a degree: university courses, volunteer work, finding friends to spend time with, cultivating new friends, evenings at church. She who'd been enviably self-sufficient before Robbie was born, and totally absorbed in Robbie after he'd been born, was now desperate for any sort of companionship however haphazard and transient.

Even, sometimes, her mother's companionship. Whit could not quite comprehend.

When Whit came home, immediately he went to his computer. A kind of gravitational force pulled him to it, as into a black hole—as Dinah ruefully observed. All day, when he wasn't engaged in work at the radio station, or meetings with people, he was obsessed with his e-mail and cell phone which he might check a dozen times an hour.

An hour?—the scale was rather more to the minute.

Like one who has come to consciousness in a devastated city, amid ruins, he would find a way of surviving, a primitive shelter.

Here, I can live. I can breathe, here.

Hadn't meant to speak harshly to the woman.

He never did. And mostly, they forgave him.

She was one of the wealthy donors who helped subsidize WCYS-FM. Particularly, Whit Whitcomb's *American Classics & New Age*. That is—she and her husband contributed.

At fund-raisers, the Proxmires were photographed in their gorgeous formal attire. These were occasions when Whit shook hands with Tracy Proxmire while his much-younger wife Hedy stood by smiling and beautiful.

She'd been saying to Whit that she understood, of course—he would *not ever* leave his wife.

And he'd said, You're sure of that? Wow.

And she'd said, You know, Whit—you could say there's a disadvantage to having had a personal catastrophe in your life.

And he'd said, Is there? Really? And what might that be?

And she'd said, Being unaware of the degree to which you're an asshole, because people give you a free ride.

And he'd laughed. His face stung as if the woman had slapped him, but still he laughed.

Then he said, The actual disadvantage is that you attribute your subsequent life—every mood, every downturn—to that catastrophe. You can't imagine an alternative life. There is only the *one life*. You have no perspective.

This was true. This was sad, banal, quasi-profound, *true*.

He thought, Is this the end for us? Maybe time.

With each of the women who was not Whit's companion in bereavement there came such a time.

Sometimes early, after only a few surreptitious meetings. Sometimes later, when the eager sexual yearning began to subside into something more durable.

The women seemed never to be prepared. Whit was well prepared.

Though Whit was, at the outset, the more eager lover. Like a child ravenous for affection, the warmth of touch.

Now he was trying to be gallant. Trying not to notice the woman's fingernails as she stroked his arm as if to comfort him.

Each time they'd been together the nails had been polished a different color: pale pink, pale peach, russet-red, dark lavender. Initially he'd expressed a jocular sort of admiration. Then, a subsequent time, bemusement. But more recently, a sort of embarrassment. (Were the fancy fingernails for *him*? The woman's glamour calculated and assembled for *him*?) It made him smile to think, women have such ridiculous things done to them *on purpose!*

(Except Dinah of course. Poor Dinah's nails were short, broken, splintered. The protein seemed to have leached out of her body, her nails were papery-thin.)

Today, the nails were pearly. Opalescent.

But more significantly, the nails had been reshaped, and were no longer oval but square, like tiny shovels. Whit found himself staring at them wondering how Hedy could use her hands?—for instance, with a cell phone?

Carefully Hedy said, not wanting to offend her thin-skinned lover, The perspective you lose is not knowing how different your life would be, otherwise. I mean your inner, essential life . . .

Whit wasn't sure he'd heard this correctly. He was still staring at the fingernails wondering now if something so artificial-looking could still be, in a way, natural; whether, if he tried to break off one of the nails, it wouldn't break, because it was an actual outgrowth of the woman's body.

If there was a problem in the marriage, Hedy said, unaware of Whit's mounting rage, there would still be a problem. That's *if.*

"If"—?

Well, I'm trying to make a point. Maybe it's a point that isn't viable.

That might be, Hedy.

What I'm saying is that it might be unreal, illogical, in a way unjust to blame your life on something that went terribly wrong in a point in time . . .

He left her to flounder on. He'd lost interest in the ridiculous nails if they were real or fake; or whether the woman's feeling for him was real or fake or some incalculable admixture of the two. *Trace elements*—too small to measure.

It was their time together when abruptly Whit said he had to get back home. He'd never said such a thing to Mrs. Proxmire before but he said it now, with sudden urgency.

Why? Is something waiting for you back home?

Isn't that what "home" is?—something waiting for you?

Well, you've never brought up the subject before, Whit.

So I won't, again.

A forty-five-minute drive from Ann Arbor Hills and midway, on the state highway, he heard his cell phone ringing, those heart-tripping unmistakable notes, but he refrained from answering it for he'd had more than one near-accident driving this very highway and answering calls he shouldn't have answered; and when he arrived home, there was Dinah standing on the lighted porch awaiting him.

Often, Whit didn't arrive home until late. Yet, here was Dinah awaiting him.

She was holding something in her arms, that stirred—their next-door neighbor's ginger cat. Whit waved to her as he turned into the driveway, though he felt dread. Was it Dinah who'd tried to call him? They spoke often during the day though they had *no news*. He wished, from his wife, no more news, ever.

As he opened the car door, Dinah stumbled down the porch steps. Her scarred face was quickened, her eyes alight.

"Whit! They've found Robbie."

III

ANN ARBOR, MICHIGAN
SEPTEMBER 2012

Where *was* he?

They were waiting for him in the first-floor atrium of the tinted-glass Washtenaw Building in Ann Arbor, Michigan.

After fifty minutes with Dr. Kozdoi the parents had left the therapist's office on the third floor of the building, and Robbie remained for another fifty minutes for a private session with her.

This had been their practice for the past several months, since they'd initiated counseling sessions for their son.

It was 12:12 P.M. Robbie's session with Dr. Kozdoi would have ended at about 12:00 noon.

"Do you want to go look for him? Or . . ."

"He might be in the restroom upstairs."

"We could wait a few more minutes. We shouldn't make Robbie feel that we're—*waiting*—so obviously."

Whit took Dinah's hand, and stroked it. Gently.

Dinah turned her hand, as she always did, to grasp Whit's fingers from beneath. She could feel the strength coursing through the man, her husband. She thought *We are perfect now. We are a family now.*

They decided to wait for Robbie, a few minutes longer. He was eleven years old and might like a little privacy, after his session with Dr. Kozdoi.

Your son is making *enormous progress,* Dr. Kozdoi told them.

After his unspeakable ordeal, he is doing *remarkably well.*

Robbie did not talk to his parents of his private sessions with the therapist; nor did Dr. Kozdoi tell them anything that would violate the boy's confidentiality—of course.

The Whitcombs knew that at times, unable or unwilling to speak, Robbie was given a charcoal stick to draw for Dr. Kozdoi on sheets of construction paper. But this "art" remained in Dr. Kozdoi's office and Dinah and Whit hadn't yet seen any of it.

Dinah had called Dr. Kozdoi to ask her: Has he told you anything—much—about *that man?*

(*That man* was Dinah's way of alluding to the abductor and sexual predator known to police as "Chester Cash.")

Dr. Kozdoi had replied that she could not discuss this with Dinah, just yet. If—when—the subject came up during the meeting with the three of them, that would be different.

Dinah had said, But I don't want you to tell me anything that my son has actually *said,* Dr. Kozdoi. But only if—if—he has brought up *that man . . .*

Politely Dr. Kozdoi repeated that she was very sorry, she couldn't discuss Robbie with Dinah, just yet.

Of course, the Whitcombs understood that Robbie must be speaking of *that man* to the therapist. As he'd spoken, if briefly and not always coherently, to law enforcement officials.

And eventually, he would speak of *that man* to his parents. When the time was right.

Dr. Kozdoi had told them: In such sensitive child-therapy, nothing should be hurried. Premature disclosures are counterproductive. The interrogative model is forbidden. The young patient must never feel that he is being examined, queried, doubted, "attacked" . . .

In her cheerful way Dinah had asked Robbie if he liked Dr. Kozdoi—as she did—and Robbie murmured what sounded like *Yeh she's OK.*

Whit had asked Robbie if he thought Dr. Kozdoi was helping him and Robbie murmured what sounded like *Yeh guess so.*

Robbie was not the chattering child of six years ago. This eleven-year-old Robbie was a very different boy altogether.

Difficult to encourage Robbie to *look them in the eyes.*

This Robbie was shy, soft-spoken. His reaction time, when spoken to, seemed just perceptibly delayed.

He did not smile spontaneously. His smiles were also just perceptibly delayed.

Oh, Dinah hated to remind the boy—she hated herself as a mother, in such a role—to try to stand up straight, not to slouch his shoulders, hold his head high.

She could not bring herself to say *You must not slouch and cringe. You are safe with your loving parents now.*

Yet, it was a fact: the five-year-old Robbie was not so evident in the eleven-year-old's face.

The eyes were not a child's eyes. The eyes were dark, wary and watchful.

The crudely dyed hair—bleached-blond, dirty-blond, brown— had mostly grown out. Whit had taken the boy to have the last of the dyed hair trimmed away and now dark-haired Robbie more resembled, Whit thought with satisfaction, a boy who might be *his son.*

As a little boy Robbie had called them *Mommy, Daddy. Mommy! Dad-dy!*

Countless times a day the delightful child-voice *Mom-my! Dad-dy!*

With some prompting, Robbie now called his parents *Mom, Dad.*

Such intimate words didn't come naturally to him. Not just yet.

Dinah had more than once seen a look of panic in the boy's eyes, as in the eyes of a stutterer as he approaches a particularly treacherous patch of sound.

Mom. Dad.

They hugged him often. He was so tall—for a little boy . . .

In fact, Robbie was of average height for an eleven-year-old. But he was still very thin.

His white-blood count was improving. His anemia had nearly vanished.

When Robbie was hugged he stood limp, unresisting. His thin arms at his sides.

As if he is being held captive. He will not try to escape.

His breathing quickened at such times. Heat lifted from his skin. Dinah might have imagined it, his little heart pounded.

It was somewhat hurtful to her, when Robbie was hugged by his grandmother, Geraldine, he reacted in much the same way. When he was kissed on the cheek, his eyelids fluttered.

He did not—yet—kiss in return.

Lately, encouraged by Dinah, and (perhaps) by Dr. Kozdoi, Robbie was making a gesture at hugging his parents when they hugged him, if awkwardly.

Yet, Dinah was convinced that Robbie liked being hugged, and even kissed, as he seemed to like, unexpectedly for an eleven-year-old, being assigned household tasks: when he finished one, he asked for another. Even clearing the table, rinsing dishes and putting them in the dishwasher. Even laundry. Vacuuming!

He seemed to like being praised for these tasks. If Robbie was to smile, it was at such times.

That man had treated him like a slave, the Whitcombs had learned. Among the other horrors to which he'd subjected their son for six years of his childhood.

Yet, he is our son. He is our Robbie.

We would know him anywhere.

* * *

253

It was nearly four months since the call had come to Dinah. Four months since the Whitcombs were summoned to New Jersey, to be reunited with their son.

They'd flown to Newark. Hired a car and driven to New Brunswick, to the Robert Wood Johnson Memorial children's hospital where Robbie was being treated for malnourishment, anemia, and exhaustion following an estimated forty-eight hours when he'd been lost in the foothills of the Kittatinny Mountains, east of the Delaware Water Gap.

It was two months now since the Whitcombs had moved out of their Ypsilanti house to live in Ann Arbor, at 608 Third Street, in a handsome old Victorian house leased from a University of Michigan biology professor on sabbatical abroad.

What a relief, to live in the small university town and no longer in Ypsilanti, where the Whitcombs' neighbors were overly solicitous of them—overly *interested* in them—and where they'd accumulated too many bad memories.

Ann Arbor was the most cosmopolitan university community in Michigan, if not in the Midwest. Whit joked that of the faces one saw on the streets, at least one out of three was Asian.

It was just three months since the Whitcombs began seeing Dr. Miriam Kozdoi, a highly regarded local therapist whose training in psychology was in child- and family-counseling and whose degrees were from the University of Michigan.

Dinah liked Dr. Kozdoi, very much. Whit liked her too, though with some reservations.

In the roles in which their marriage seemed to have placed them, Dinah was the optimist; Whit, the one who *doubts*.

Both the Whitcombs liked it that Dr. Kozdoi was frank, funny, unaffected, obviously very intelligent. They liked it that her conversation was filled with cultural references—books, movies, music, opera, art, TV, Internet, sports. (Dr. Kozdoi allowed it to be known that, at least until recently, she'd been an avid hiker and skier.) They admired her office which was quirkily furnished: a young patient could sit, if he wished, in a large soft chair shaped like a baseball catcher's mitt; older patients had the option of sitting in more conventional chairs. On the walls were reproductions of classic black-and-white American photography by Ansel Adams, Edward Weston, Alfred Stieglitz, Dorothea Lange, Bruce Davidson. Floor-to-ceiling bookshelves were crammed with books, magazines, professional journals that had the look of materials frequently consulted.

The atmosphere of the office was one of relaxation, trust. An antique grandfather clock softly struck the half hour. Dr. Kozdoi sat, not at a desk, but at a pale-green plastic table with curved corners. But there was the square box of tissues on the table, in an ebony container, prominent as it had been in the offices of therapists whom Dinah had seen, over the years.

Please take a tissue. There is nothing wrong with a few tears.

Dr. Kozdoi herself was a tall stout smiling woman with graying hair cut short as a man's, yet with fluffy bangs falling to her eyebrows, and ornate hand-tooled silver earrings. She wore exotic Indian and Chinese shawls over her plain-cut trouser suits. If Whit liked her less than Dinah did, it was perhaps because Dr. Kozdoi wasn't so *feminine* a woman, and yet her gaze was hypnotic to him, mesmerizing.

In the family-therapy session, Whit spoke less than Dinah did. And Robbie hardly spoke at all.

Since meeting Dr. Kozdoi, who was highly recommended to Dinah by one of her former psychology professors, Dinah began wearing conspicuous earrings also. She'd realized—it was a way of distracting attention from her face!

She'd seen how searchingly Dr. Kozdoi had looked at her, at their initial meeting. How warmly, and firmly, Dr. Kozdoi had taken her hand, and held it.

The woman had understood, Dinah thought: she'd known how repulsive Dinah felt, how sad, how embarrassed for her husband and her son, how *unfeminine;* yet how determined Dinah was, to acknowledge none of this.

Keep my secret for me. Please!

For the weekly meetings with Dr. Kozdoi, Dinah never failed to dress attractively. Not her usual well-laundered jeans, nor even her black nylon "dressy" slacks—but rather dresses, skirts. And shawls, less colorful than Dr. Kozdoi's shawls. Since Robbie's return she'd been taking much more interest in her appearance, shampooing her hair often, and wearing lipstick. She'd even tried putting makeup on her face, covering some of the scars with powder. Maybe, in less than full-frontal daylight, the optical illusion was a success.

Happy. My life is restored to me!

And my health too. Or nearly.

Dinah still walked with difficulty, though rarely now serious difficulty. She had not *fallen* for years.

(And if she did lose her balance, slip and fall inside the house, who would know? She would never tell Whit and so far, fortunately, Robbie had never observed her.)

Dinah had several times seen an expression of pained sympathy in her son's eyes, when he looked at her.

He'd been informed—he'd had to be informed—that his mother had "minor disabilities" as a consequence of *that man* who'd abducted him and tried to murder her with his minivan. Whit thought it was imperative that Robbie know this fact.

Dinah wouldn't have told him. She didn't think so.

Yet later she thought it had been a good idea. For now Robbie knew all the more how she'd loved him in that long-ago time he could barely recall. Maybe he wouldn't be embarrassed of having a mother with a face *not quite right.*

(It wasn't clear if Robbie remembered anything of his early childhood or whether he gave vague answers shaped by what adults wanted him to say. When police officers had first interviewed him the previous May, after he'd been hospitalized, he hadn't seemed to know even his name of that time—"Gideon Cash.")

Dinah wanted to think *He isn't embarrassed of his mother, that I am a freak. He feels closer to me than he feels to Whit.*

Dinah spent more time with Robbie than Whit did, of necessity. Whit had cut down on his work when Robbie had first returned to them, but after two months he'd returned to his previous schedule.

Your father is a very busy man. People adore him!

Perhaps this wasn't altogether true. "Whit" Whitcomb had numerous enemies in Ypsilanti–Ann Arbor, radio listeners who disliked his *left-wing politics* and resented his local high profile. He'd even received hate mail, some of it jeering and vengeful, when law enforcement authorities in New Jersey had reunited him with his abducted son, and both local and national media had covered the story.

Dinah had a new life now, driving a car, taking her son to medical and dental appointments; walking with him in the university arboretum; taking him to a summer course under the auspices of the University of Michigan Education School, where along with other children his age who had disabilities or whose academic schooling had been interrupted, he would complete the equivalent of seventh grade in the State of Michigan. In New Jersey, as "Gideon Cash," Robbie had received nearly uniform high grades from his teachers; but in the six-week summer session he seemed to be distracted and to have difficulty concentrating, and didn't make friends with the other students.

The friendly young woman instructor had known who "Robbie Whitcomb" was—of course. Her eyes meeting Dinah's eyes had told all. *I know. Oh I am so sorry!—but I will keep your secret.* Dinah had smiled, stiffly.

Dinah had not told anyone, yet Dinah didn't intend to live a life of paranoid secrecy, either.

Ypsilanti–Ann Arbor constituted a relatively small community. By the summer of 2012, everyone knew who *Robbie Whitcomb* and his parents *Dinah and Whit* were.

The story of the abduction, the "six-year captivity," the release from captivity and the reunifying of the family in New Jersey had been covered repeatedly, in exhaustive and often lurid detail. The Whitcombs had agreed to give a single press conference in early June, at WCYS-FM headquarters; Robbie had not been present, and the only photos provided of him were of his five-year-old self, that had appeared on the MISSING CHILD poster.

Many follow-up stories had been aired, on national cable channels, focusing upon the *serial killer sex predator "Chester Cash"* who'd allegedly kidnapped several young boys and murdered and buried at least three of them in a wilderness area near his Kittatinny Falls, New Jersey, home. Photographs of the other boys—such young, beautiful boys!—had been displayed, and among them Robbie's young face; but Robbie had not been one of the *murder victims.*

The Whitcombs had nothing to do with these stories and refused to be interviewed for them. Grimly Whit watched such stories for he felt that, as Robbie's father, he should know as much as he could; but Dinah hid away, appalled.

(Whit taped the programs and saw them late at night. When Robbie was safely in bed, and asleep.)

(At least, it was his parents' assumption, after they put him to bed, hugging, kissing him, pulling bedclothes up to his chin, that Robbie slept.)

*   *   *

In their household, Dinah was calm, placating and good-natured—as befitted a handicapped person with a Hallowe'en face. (This was Dinah's sense of humor, from which Robbie was mostly spared.)

In their household, Whit was likely to be the more emotional parent, flaring up in anger at the unwanted attentions of others, determined to protect his son and wife from media exploitation.

(Whit had more than once knocked smartphones out of hands, to prevent pictures or videos taken of his family when they were out together. How Dinah coped with this phenomenon, if she coped with it at all, Dinah didn't tell Whit.)

When Dinah took Robbie to his summer class, she'd waited for him in the neighborhood of small shops, secondhand bookstores and boutiques at the edge of the university campus; she'd walked along the sidewalks, slowly, savoring even the pain in her legs and lower back, thinking with pleasure that it was *her son* she was waiting for, to drive back home.

She hoped that, glancing at her, people could tell. *A mother, and soon she'll be picking up her child. Look how happy she is!*

Often Dinah waited for Robbie in a bookstore café. He would join her after class and they'd have a light lunch together in the café or at a nearby organic restaurant—strictly vegetarian food. It had developed that Robbie disliked meat, that meat and coarse foods like pizza made his stomach feel "sick."

In the hospital in New Brunswick, Robbie had had to be fed through a tube, for a while. Then he'd been able to eat only soft foods. Only gradually had his ability to digest normal foods returned. But meat, he said, was "nasty."

By degrees, Robbie had come to like yogurt, fruit smoothies, shredded wheat, muesli, sautéed tofu, jasmine rice, brown rice, wild rice, and all varieties of pasta. His desserts were carrot cake, gingerbread, strawberries, banana smoothies, frozen yogurt. His parents introduced him to Chinese, Thai, Middle Eastern and Indian cuisine, which featured many vegetarian dishes. Dinah was trying to convert him from carbonated soda drinks to the Snapple drinks which she preferred and which were far healthier.

Robbie knew of organic foods. Robbie began to look for *organic* on food labels.

His parents were pleased with this. (Were they? Dinah was pleased.) Except they worried, their son had a tendency to be— well, just slightly—if you lived with him intimately, and observed him up close—*compulsive.*

Dinah remembered: the parking-lot game. How she'd asked Robbie to be responsible for remembering where their car was parked, and how terribly serious Robbie had been. As if, unknowing, Dinah had triggered some mechanism in his child-brain, that had had a result she hadn't anticipated.

Now, he is no longer a child. He has grown up. Yet he must be shielded.

*   *   *

Of course, Dinah no longer smoked. Even in secret.

She had not smoked a cigarette—at least, an entire cigarette—since late that afternoon of April 11, 2006.

It was a filthy habit. She was deeply ashamed she'd ever smoked in her son's presence.

Despite his distractions, and difficulties with sleeping a normal seven-hour night, Robbie did well in the summer session. He was enrolled in Ann Arbor Middle School, in seventh grade; the first day of classes was next Tuesday, after Labor Day.

Dinah's mother had pleaded with her to bring her family to Birmingham, to live with her in her five-bedroom Colonial on Bayberry Drive. Instead of moving from Ypsilanti to Ann Arbor, they could move in with her, and Robbie could attend Birmingham Day School, to which Geraldine would send him.

You owe it to your son, Geraldine said, to try to protect him. In Ypsilanti and Ann Arbor, everyone knew too much about the Whitcombs. In Birmingham, people were more discreet.

Dinah doubted this. Dinah doubted that there was anywhere in the Midwest, or anywhere in the country, where the name "Whitcomb" wasn't known by this time.

There had been a cover feature in *People*. On CBS-TV *48 Hours Mystery*, a feature on "Chester Cash, Serial Sex Predator and Murderer."

Much had been made in the popular media of the fact that during his six years as a captive of Chester Cash, Robbie hadn't attempted to escape, evidently, or to call attention to his captivity.

Even when his captor was forcing him to spend hours in the *safety-box,* and continued to sexually abuse him, and torture him; even after his captor had brought another boy, an eight-year-old, into the household, the child known as "Gideon Cash" had not rebelled.

Why hadn't the boy told someone at his school? A teacher, a friend? Why hadn't he gone to police officers in Kittatinny Falls? Why hadn't he tried to run away? Six years.

There was no answer to this question. Dinah did not allow herself to think of any answer.

She and Whit did not discuss this. *Unless you'd lived the hell that Robbie had lived, you could not know. And you could not judge.*

Hateful things had been said in the media and online. Dinah knew, without being certain. She had ceased using the Internet except for the weather forecast, recipes, a book club. She would no more have typed in *Robbie Whitcomb* than she'd have swallowed a mouthful of glass, she'd told Whit.

Whit shielded her from such things, and Dinah had no wish to be enlightened.

Geraldine persisted: "It would be so much healthier for all of you to make a fresh start. In a new community. Whit has been with that public radio station for most of his adult life. He should get another job—a more stable job. One that doesn't depend upon listeners' polls and contributions."

There was the not-so-subtle hint that Geraldine would help Dinah's family, financially. This was an insult!—though Dinah knew her mother only meant well.

Dinah hadn't mentioned her mother's suggestions to Whit. She'd known how he would have reacted. How wounded and indignant he'd have been, and how furious.

Tell your mother to leave us alone. Permanently.

Dinah had thanked her mother, and declined.

Geraldine said, "You might be making a mistake, Dinah. To stay in that part of Michigan." She'd come close to saying, to stay with *him.*

"It's a mistake we will have to live with, Mother. If you're ashamed of us, we can't help that."

"I'm not *ashamed* of you, Dinah! I love you."

But we don't love you. We don't need you, we have each other.

Dinah had driven Robbie to the school, which was about two miles from their house on Third Street. They'd parked, and walked around the building. Dinah had felt Robbie's mounting excitement—she'd wished to think it was excitement and not anxiety or dread.

"It looks like a very nice school, Robbie." Dinah spoke enthusiastically as often she did to Robbie, without the expectation of Robbie replying. "Everyone has told us, teachers here are excellent."

This was true. And when Dinah had enrolled Robbie, she'd been impressed with the administrative and teaching staff she'd met.

Dr. Kozdoi too had good things to say about the school. But Dr. Kozdoi was, by her admission, a firm believer in public education.

She thought, too, that Robbie would make a good adjustment to school in Ann Arbor, among the children of ethnic minority families. Their interest in lurid tabloid stories would be minimal, Dr. Kozdoi thought.

Ever more, Dr. Kozdoi was becoming a member of the Whitcomb family. Her (invisible) presence was enhancing. Weekly sessions in her office had become crucial to Dinah and Whit for in these, their relationship with each other was a constant issue; each was determined, for Robbie's sake as well as for theirs, that their relationship be presented in the best possible way.

Dinah acknowledged—*Maybe I'm too verbal—too enthusiastic! Maybe this tires people out.*

Whit acknowledged—*Maybe I'm too skeptical—pessimistic about the world.*

Neither would have acknowledged—*Somehow, our love has turned into something else. Guilt?*

By degrees, Whit was coming to respect Dr. Kozdoi. He'd taken to calling her Robbie's "good" grandmother.

To his admirers, "Whit" Whitcomb had visibly changed since his son had returned to his life. Whit had shaved off his beard, trimmed his shaggy hair, was looking almost *corporate.*

(And why? It was a secret.)

(Not even Dinah knew: Whit had resolved to shave off his beard as soon as he'd seen photographs of "Chester Cash," at that time in police custody in New Jersey. The man's whiskered jaws, his shoulder-length hair, his swaggering-hippie pretensions.

How appalled Whit had been, the sex predator–murderer resembled *him*.)

(Most stunning to Whit, he believed he'd once met Chester
Cash in the fall of 2001 after the terrorist attacks of 9/11; Whit
had been involved in an Ann Arbor–Detroit community outreach program called Hands Across Borders, held on the Wayne
State University campus, where a number of community leaders
spoke, and among these was the charismatic "Reverend Cash"
who'd been associated with the small, African-American Church
of Abiding Hope in center city, Detroit. Whit had disliked the
man for his pseudo-modest Christly manner—for his bristling
beard and "piercing" eyes. After Whit had spoken to the rally,
Reverend Cash had come to him, to shake his hand . . . Whit's
memory dissolved at this point, in a tremulous amnesia like
fine white mist.)

(Whit could not bear it—he could not allow himself to think
it—that he might have shaken hands with the madman who
would, within a few years, abduct Whit's own son, and keep
him captive for six years.)

Dinah couldn't help but think that Robbie felt more com-
fortable with his mother than with his father who was always
smiling at him—at least, with his mouth-muscles.

A smile is aggressive, Dinah thought. A smile demands a
response.

Clearly it was hard for Robbie to smile in return. To smile
upon demand. Whit needed to be less conspicuously *trying to
love their son*.

With her damaged face, Dinah had become skilled at smiling in just the right way, at the right time. She might smile at strangers, to reassure them that, yes she knew she was disfigured: but yes, it was all right. She didn't smile so often at Robbie because she knew it made him uneasy, like a mirror thrust too close against his face.

It was crucial to Dinah, that Robbie know how she'd loved him, and had tried to keep him from being taken from her. The extent of her injuries was inconsequential set beside this fact. Dinah had seen her son stare at her, during therapy sessions, when this subject had come up. She'd seen the look in his eyes— *My mother almost died for me. My mother must have loved me.*

Tears welled in her eyes. She'd groped for a tissue from out of Dr. Kozdoi's square tissue-box.

When Dinah had first seen their son, in the hospital in New Brunswick, she'd been astonished at the sight of the boy—his lean face, his small concave broken-looking chest, his grave eyes and wounded mouth. Yet, he was so *grown*. He wasn't a child but a *boy*.

It made her sick and faint, to think that they'd lost six years of their son's childhood. Six years of their own young lives.

That man had stolen a part of their souls from them. No punishment, not even death, could compensate for that loss.

"I believe in capital punishment now. I could inject the poison myself, I think."

Hotly Dinah had said this to Whit, just once. Whit had said, "I could kill him with my bare hands."

But there was no point in such thoughts, Dinah knew. Her yoga, her meditations, her slow healing walks while Robbie was in summer school, had led her to this conclusion.

"Yet, I could never 'forgive' him. My God!"

Dinah had spoken aloud. Whit frowned at her but didn't ask what she'd said.

Whit too was captivated by his own thoughts. Like runaway horses dragging him in their wake, no matter how he was injured, exhausted.

We are so very happy to have our son back.

Yet, it is so very tiring. Each hour of each day.

Waiting for—what?

They were waiting to hear if the man known as "Chester Cash" would plead guilty to the long list of charges brought against him, or whether, abetted by a *pro bono* defense lawyer in hope of acquiring nationwide notoriety, he would plead "not guilty."

In which case there would be a trial in the State of Michigan, in Washtenaw County, where Robbie Whitcomb had been abducted. And there would be a trial in the State of New Jersey, in Lenape County, where Robbie Whitcomb had been held captive and many times assaulted in the years 2006 to 2012.

It was likely that, if these trials were held, there would be other, separate trials in which Chester Cash would be tried for murder as well as kidnapping, assault, and keeping an individual, a minor, against his will. So far, the bodies of three boys had been discovered in a wilderness area approximately a mile from Cash's Kittatinny Falls property.

And there was eight-year-old Kendall McCane, abducted from his family's home in Toms River, New Jersey, on May 26, 2012, and found in a "locked box the size of a casket" in Cash's minivan, by Indiana police. For this abduction, assault, and enforced captivity, Cash would be tried, too.

The middle-aged children of Myrna Helmerich, Cash's deceased wife, were pressing Mercer County, New Jersey, authorities to exhume their mother's body which was buried in a cemetery in Grindell Park, a residential neighborhood in Trenton. Their claim was that her "husband" Chester Cash had surely murdered her, and made the death look like heart failure, in order to collect her insurance money, and inherit her estate.

There had not been anything like the Chester Cash story in New Jersey for decades. Major networks as well as the cable channels had been covering the case intermittently since late May. Cash himself was being held without bail in a segregated unit of the Lenape County men's detention center.

Only through Cash's loquacious lawyer Cheyenne Brady were bulletins regularly released to the media, that, as his client Reverend Cash was "innocent" of the charges brought against him, it would not be possible for him to plead "guilty."

Robbie had been found by hikers wandering in a desolate area in the Kittatinny Mountains. According to his confused account, he'd been lost for two days and two nights. He'd said that someone was "after" him—"wanted to hurt him." He'd been exhausted, staggering, incoherent. He'd been unable to walk without assistance and so the hikers had called for medical assistance, carrying the boy to a nearby road.

He'd been transported to the nearest ER, in Clinton, New Jersey. From there, as his condition deteriorated, to the Robert Wood Johnson children's hospital in New Brunswick where, for a brief while, he'd been put on a respirator and fed through a feeding tube.

He'd suffered from severe dehydration, malnutrition, anemia, and shock. His blood pressure had plummeted to fifty-nine over sixty and his heartbeat had accelerated wildly.

Old injuries, wounds and scars had been discovered on every part of the boy's body as well as in and around his genitals and his anus.

In the hospital, the boy had been questioned when he was well enough to speak, but he hadn't seemed to know his name, or where he was from; he was thought to be an abused child, abandoned by his parent or parents, mentally retarded or schizophrenic. Then, after a few days, when his condition had stabilized, he'd told child welfare officers that he'd "run away" from a man who had "trapped" him in a house on the Saw Mill Road in Kittatinny Falls.

He'd said that the man was "angry" with him and "wanted to kill" him.

He'd said that the man had made him carry a shovel out into the mountains—"It was time for me to die, I guess. I would have to dig the hole and he would bury me with his other sons."

When the boy was asked if the man was his father he'd said "Yes"—but then, later, he'd said "No."

Asked who the man was he'd hesitated and said, "Daddy Love."

Daddy Love? But what was the man's name?

The boy shook his head, mutely.

But where are your parents? he was asked.

His parents had "given him away," he said. He didn't know where they lived or who they were and the man had told him that they were dead now—"And gone to Hell that was God's punishment."

As soon as the nameless boy's photograph appeared on New Jersey television channels, viewers in Kittatinny Falls called police to identify him as "Gideon Cash" who'd lived with his father "Chester Cash" on a farm on the Saw Mill Road.

A warrant was issued for the arrest of Chester Cash. When New Jersey state police arrived at the farmhouse, however, the house was empty. There was no vehicle on the premises, and inside the house it looked as if someone had departed hurriedly.

Through a national missing-children data base, "Robbie Whitcomb" was identified: a five-year-old who'd been abducted from the Libertyville Mall in Ypsilanti, Michigan, in April 2006. A call was made to the child's parents, who lived still in the house in Ypsilanti, and had the same telephone numbers.

A nationwide search was initiated for "Chester Cash" who was arrested a few days later, at 2 A.M. on I-70 near Terre Haute,

Indiana; Indiana state troopers had sighted the Chrysler minivan, which matched the description of the wanted man's vehicle and which had been observed "weaving" on the highway as if the driver was lapsing in and out of consciousness. Flagged over onto the shoulder of the road by the officer, Chester Cash had stumbled from the van and tried to run, was apprehended and thrown down onto the ground and handcuffed.

To their astonishment police officers discovered in the back of the van, in a wooden box resembling a casket, with a locked lid, a young boy in a semiconscious state, severely dehydrated; he was taken to a local ER, and soon identified as eight-year-old Kendall McCane of Toms River, New Jersey, whose parents had reported him missing from the backyard of their home several days before.

Much was made in the media of the state troopers' surprise and disgust at having found a captive little boy in the "box like a casket"—"like something out of a horror movie except worse, it was *real*."

Kittatinny Falls residents who'd known Chester Cash and his son Gideon told police that Chet Cash had always seemed "normal enough"—they guessed. He'd said that the boy's mother had died—they'd moved to New Jersey from Maine, unless it was Michigan. Cash had liked to hang out with "other fathers" when he encountered them, for instance at a softball game or a barbecue, or at church. Cash had rarely let the boy out of his sight when they were together; he'd refused to allow the boy to ride the school bus, and never let him visit the homes of his classmates. Yet more recently, in past months, the boy was often seen bicycling along country roads and in town, alone. You got the impression, neighbors named McIntyre said disapprovingly, that the boy was "neglected."

All were shocked by the revelation that there'd been two captive boys in the farm on the Saw Mill Road.

Since he'd tried to run from state police in Indiana, and since his arrest and extradition to New Jersey, Chester Cash had refused to speak to police. He was exercising, as he said, his *right to remain silent.*

Through his lawyer Cheyenne Brady, who'd given numerous interviews to the insatiable twenty-four-hour news channels, it was being claimed that Chet Cash was a "devout Christian minister, a man of God" who'd "rescued" boys from abusive parents; he'd "rescued" little Robbie Whitcomb from a "bad mother," and the boy had been "grateful" to live with him. This would be Cash's defense at his trial—"My client acknowledges that he 'acted outside of the secular law'—in accordance with a 'higher moral law.' Reverend Cash is 'not guilty' of forcible abduction and the other charges because he is 'not guilty' of violating this higher law."

It would be a nightmare, the Whitcombs thought, if Cash insisted upon a trial—insisted upon his "innocence." A nightmare if their sensitive son was forced to testify against his abductor and rapist. His captor-torturer for six years.

A nightmare if their son was forced to relive even a part of those horrific six years.

"God won't let this happen, I think. God has restored Robbie to us, He will not punish Robbie and us further."

So Dinah spoke, in a way that disturbed and infuriated her husband.

"If I could just kill him with my bare hands. *That* would be a very generous gesture of God."

So Whit said. Clenching and unclenching his fists.

It was 12:19 P.M. by Whit's digital watch. And still Robbie hadn't appeared on the stairway or on the third floor which was open above the atrium where he might have waved to his parents below, over the railing.

"Maybe you could check out the restrooms? Or maybe—Dr. Kozdoi's office . . ."

"He wouldn't be with her this long, Dinah. Or if he was, Dr. Kozdoi would have called to tell us where he is."

It was their custom after these sessions with Dr. Kozdoi for the family to have lunch together, at one or another nearby restaurant. At such times Dinah and Whit spoke expansively, and Robbie sat silently, eyes downcast. His parents' sessions with Dr. Kozdoi left them excited, if not elated; Robbie's sessions with Dr. Kozdoi left him more reticent than usual.

What is he thinking? Is he—remembering?
But what is he remembering?

Whit took the elevator to the third floor, to check out the men's restroom there. Then, he'd check out the second floor. And finally, the first floor.

Once, a few weeks ago, when Robbie hadn't appeared after his session with Dr. Kozdoi, Whit had gone to look for him and had found him in the third-floor men's room.

That is, Whit had entered the restroom and heard an anguished muffled sound, as of sobbing, in one of the toilet stalls.

He'd heard, too, what sounded like physical distress. Gastrointestinal distress, diarrhea. His son was suffering, on the toilet in that stall, but his son would wish to suffer in private, Whit knew. So he'd retreated, returned to the atrium to wait with Dinah for their son to join them.

He'd told Dinah that Robbie was in the men's room. Nothing serious, and he'd be joining them in a few minutes.

This had been the case. When Robbie came down the stairs, slowly, like a boy in a dream, white-faced, holding himself stiffly, he'd seemed to be seeing his parents for a while, without recognizing them; then, he'd lifted his hand in a boyish sort of salute.

Hi Mom. Dad.

His voice was small, flat, mechanical. His eyes were evasive.

Dinah had bit her lower lip, and gone to Robbie to hug him, wordlessly.

Hey Mom. I'm OK.

His hands smelled of soap. Vigorously he'd washed them in the restroom.

Another time, Whit had found Robbie on the third floor, but this time not in the men's room. He'd been crouched in a corner at the far end of the corridor, his head lowered onto his knees and his face hidden as if he was sleeping, or very tired. When Whit approached cautiously, Robbie had shuddered, as if sensing someone's approach; but he hadn't looked up, and when Whit squatted to speak to him, and to hug him, he hadn't reacted for several seconds.

Hi Dad. I'm OK.

Now as Whit took the elevator to the third floor, Dinah wandered out of the atrium and along a corridor, to the foyer at the front of the building. The Washtenaw Building housed medical and professional offices and suites; it was only a few years old, made of dark-tinted glass and aluminum. On this weekday morning in early September, there were many visitors including individuals in wheelchairs; among them, a woman younger than Dinah, with a twisted spine, a small fixed smile, a companion who might have been a brother, or a husband. Dinah smiled nervously at the woman who glanced past her without seeing her.

Dinah exited the building through revolving doors. The outdoor air was surprisingly hot, oppressive, after the air-conditioned interior. But Dinah shivered in the warm air, that pressed against her lungs.

I am so very happy. God has blessed us.

276

She wasn't a believer, really. She attended church services only infrequently. Yet it seemed to her that, if there was a God, this God had had mercy on her, at last.

Mercy on her and Whit, returning their son to them.

Returning *their son* to them. The boy who was *theirs.*

In prisons and in detention centers, child-murderers like Chester Cash were frequently killed by fellow inmates. Throats slashed in showers. He might die, before a trial. God's mercy might prevail.

Daddy Love their son had called him. This was in one of the statements Robbie had given to police, a videotaped testimony that Dinah had not seen, but Whit had described to her.

Daddy Love! She prayed that God would prevail in His mercy and justice.

Along a paved path Dinah wandered, not remembering what she was doing, where she was and for whom she was looking; then, recalling, she found herself at the rear of the Washtenaw Building, in the beating sun. It was not true, that Dinah Whitcomb was *well:* in her soul, she was *very sick.* The man who called himself Daddy Love had perceived this—had he?

To the left was a parking lot; to the right, an outdoor café, that opened into the building, and into the atrium. She would re-enter the atrium, to wait for Whit to return with Robbie; she was in no hurry, for she didn't want to arrive before Whit and Robbie, which would be unsettling to her.

Making her way around tables on the outdoor terrace, seeing the eyes of strangers drift onto her, and snag, slightly—(is something wrong with that woman?)—Dinah saw, or thought she saw—in fact, she was seeing—a boy who resembled Robbie, sitting on a ledge, out of the sunshine. A few feet away at one of the round wrought-iron tables on the terrace, a man was sitting; at first, Dinah wanted to think that this was Whit, but of course it was not. The stranger was playfully straddling his chair, to face the boy, to whom he was speaking. He wore khaki shorts, a sleeveless T-shirt that showed his biceps and muscled shoulders; his legs were muscular, and very hairy; on his feet, flip-flops. He was in his forties perhaps, with a genial sunburnt face, a light stubble on his jaws, and on his head a Detroit Tigers baseball cap turned jauntily to the side.

Dinah's heart stopped: she saw.

The man was speaking to Robbie in a friendly way. Very likely, he was asking friendly questions. He was not menacing. Robbie might have been listening to him, though Robbie wasn't looking at him. Instead, Robbie sat hunched over a paper plate in his lap, eating hungrily.

Had the man bought Robbie some food? Or given him his own?

The man offered Robbie a sip of water from a plastic bottle. Robbie shook his head in a quick curt way that was familiar to Dinah for she'd seen it so many times—*No thanks.*

On shaky legs Dinah approached. She prayed, dear God don't let my knee give out now!

Now Robbie saw her, glancing up. He was eating a hamburger, or maybe a cheeseburger; his lips were greasy, and there was a smear of ketchup on his chin which he wiped quickly away with the back of his hand.

Unobtrusively, the man in the baseball cap slipped away from his chair, and exited the café without a backward glance.

Robbie said, in his small flat voice, swiping at his mouth now with a crumpled paper napkin, squinting-smiling at her: "Hi Mom."